This book belongs to

_____

Children's
POOLBEG

Patsy O

Ryan MacMahon

"Patsy-O and His Wonderful Pets" published 1970
by E. P. Dutton (USA) and 1972 by Richard Sadler Ltd.
"Patsy-O Goes to Spain"
and
"High in the Sky with Patsy-O"
first published 1989 by
Poolbeg Press Ltd.
Knocksedan House,
Swords, Co. Dublin, Ireland.

This book is published with the assistance of
The Arts Council/An Chomhairle Ealaíon, Ireland

ISBN I-85371-036-9

Cover design by Steven Hope
Illustrated by Steven Hope
Typeset by Print-Forme
62 Santry Close, Dublin 9.
Printed by The Guernsey Press Ltd.,
Vale, Guernsey, Channel Islands.

Patsy-O

Bryan MacMahon

Children's
POOLBEG

Bryan MacMahon is one of Ireland's most distinguished writers. He has written many poems, ballads, plays, novels and collections of short stories. His historical pageant about Ireland ran for over a year in a castle in Clare. He lives in Listowel, County Kerry.

Contents

For All My Grandchildren

Patsy-O and His Wonderful Pets

Patsy-O and His Wonderful Pets

hat's your name?" passers-by would ask the little lad.

"Patsy-O," he would always say. Though whether his full name was Patsy O'Sullivan or Patsy O'Donnell or Patsy O'Shea or Patsy O'Connor no one ever knew.

Patsy-O lived with his widowed mother and his wee sister Ita in a trim thatched cottage on the edge of a great bay on the coast of Kerry in Ireland.

Behind the little house the mountain stood on tiptoe as if to touch the clouds.

Beside the cottage grew fuchsia bushes with blossoms like red and purple bells.

In front of the door was a beach of golden sand where the waves were forever tumbling.

"Hoo!" the waves said as they rose. "Whoosh!" they said as they fell and broke.

3

"Hiss!" they said as they raced along the golden sand.

"Are you lonely, Patsy-O summer visitors to the beach would ask the boy.

"Not a bit of it!" Patsy-O would answer with a laugh. "I have my mother and my sister Ita as company. And I have my five wonderful pets."

"What pets?" the visitors wanted to know.

"Snip-Snip the Cricket, and Banjo the Cat, and Break o' Day the Cock, and Liberator the Donkey, and Rusty Red the Irish Setter."

"Well, well!" the people would say.

Then they would go off to bathe and picnic in the little cove below the cottage.

Patsy-O's father was dead. In his day he had been a clever carpenter to whom the country-folk came for tables and chairs and cartwheels.

They came also for three-legged stools on which the women sat as they were milking their wee black Kerry cows.

But the carpenter's workshop behind the cottage had been closed for many years.

When Patsy-O peered through the grimy, latticed windows he could see only cobwebs hanging from wall to wall.

And when the boy asked his mother

about the workshop she sighed deeply and said nothing.

Patsy-O called the green cricket Snip-Snip. This was exactly the sound the cricket made as it rubbed its wings together.

Patsy-O had never seen the little insect which lived in a crack in the wall at the back of the open hearth. But he had often peeped in and spied its bright green eye. And by the way the cricket looked at him Patsy-O knew that it was his friend.

Patsy-O called his marmalade-coloured cat Banjo. This was because the cat had a habit of plucking the spokes of Patsy-O's bicycle with its claws. Then it sounded as if the cat were really playing a banjo!

He called the black-and-gold-coloured cock Break o' Day. This was because every morning at daybreak when the rooster woke up in the ivy bush where he had spent the night, he would begin to call out, "Hurrah! Hurrah! It's break o' day."

At least that's what Patsy-O thought the cock was saying, although Ita said he was really saying "Cock-a-doodle-doo!"

Patsy-O called the brown donkey Liberator. This was because no matter how tightly he shut the door of the donkey's stable each evening the rascal was somehow able to free himself in the morning.

And he called the floppy-eared, bushy-tailed Irish setter Rusty Red because the dog's coat was as red as rust.

Each day in the cottage was happier then the day before. This is how each day began.

As dawn showed in the little window the cricket was first awake.

"Snip-Snip!" it would call out and wake Banjo who was lying sound asleep on the flag on the hearth. Stretching his long leg, Banjo would go off to the pantry and play the bicycle spokes.

The sound of the music would wake Break o' Day in the ivy bush. The cock would then call out, "Hurrah! Hurrah! It's break o' day."

This call would rouse out Liberator.

The donkey would put his hairy head over the half door of his stable and draw the bolt with his whiskery lips. Then he would give a great hee-haw to greet the rising sun.

All this noise, of course, would awaken Rusty Red in his kennel. The dog would leap out and begin to bark loudly.

Hearing all this commotion, Patsy-O's mother would get up and light the fire of peat or turf.

When the fire was lighting merrily she would call the children.

Patsy-O loved each and every one of his pets very dearly.

Perhaps he liked Rusty Red just a little bit more than the rest. This was because Rusty Red was faithful and devoted to his master.

On winter days Patsy-O would climb half-way up the snowy mountainside. Under his arm he would carry a large metal tray. Rusty Red would go romping beside him.

Patsy-O would place the tray flat on the snow and sit on it as if it were a sledge.

Then he would shout, "Turn your brush, Rusty Red! Rusty Red, turn your brush!"

When the red setter had turned right about, Patsy-O would grip the dog's tail gently but firmly with his two hands.

Then he would say: "Hie for home, Rusty Red! Rusty Red, hie for home!" Barking with joy the dog would scamper down the mountain slope, giving his master a jolly slide behind him.

In summertime when the sun was shining brilliantly, Patsy-O would take off his clothes and put on his bathing trunks. Then he would dash into the sea.

Barking with joy Rusty Red would follow his

master. When the water was up to his waist, Patsy-O would say, "Turn your brush, Rusty Red! Rusty Red, turn your brush!"

Swimming in the blue-green water beside the boy, the setter would turn right about.

Gently but firmly Patsy-O would grip the dog's tail and shout: "Hie for home, Rusty Red! Rusty Red, hie for home!"

Drawing his master behind him Rusty Red would swim right up to the edge of the beach.

Seeing this, the visitors would say that Rusty Red was really a very intelligent dog. Sometimes they would even pat his head.

But Rusty Red would suddenly shake himself and give the visitors a shower bath.

They didn't mind this, however. They just laughed, for they knew that Rusty Red did it for fun.

So everyone in the little cottage at the edge of the cove was as happy and as happy and as happy as the days are long. But sometimes, of course, things change. And this is exactly what happened.

One day, Patsy-O returned from the bog leading Liberator who was bearing on his back twin panniers of turf or peat.

Rusty Red was barking and running before them.

Reaching the cottage Patsy-O found Break o' Day looking down sadly from the ivy bush. He also noticed Banjo asleep in the sun with one sad eye open and the other sad eye shut. Snip-snip was silent.

Patsy-O entered the kitchen. He found his mother and sister in tears.

"What is the matter, mother?" Patsy-O asked.

"Oh," said his mother, drying her eyes, "the savings your father set aside for us before he died are now almost spent. We have only enough money to last for a few months. Then, Patsy-O, I really do not know what is to become of us."

"Cheer up, mother," Patsy-O said. "Tomorrow morning I will go into the workshop and find my father's tools. I will take to the road and seek my fortune. I will work hard and save my money. No matter how far from home I shall go, I will return on Christmas Eve to light the tall white candle on the kitchen window-sill."

The mother looked at Patsy-O with eyes filled with pride.

Ita too forgot her sorrow and began to smile.

Then the mother said: "You are a brave boy. If you wish to seek your fortune in the wide world I shall have just enough money to last me until your return on Christmas Eve to light the tall white candle on the kitchen windowsill."

The following morning Patsy-O placed the key in the rusty lock on the workshop door.

The door opened with a squeaking, creaking sound.

For the first time, Patsy-O entered the workshop where for many years his father had laboured. His mother and Ita came close behind him.

Together they broke the hammocks of cobwebs that stretched from side to side of the workshop.

Ita it was who found her father's fibre hold-all which he had called his bast. Carefully wrapped in sacking, it was hidden under the workbench. In the bast were the tools of the carpenter's trade.

Patsy-O was pleased to find that the tools had been well greased and were not a bit rusty.

As he handled the tools, he felt brave and strong as his father had been.

His mother smiled as she said:

"First let me tell you the names of the tools. This is a chisel, and this is a saw, and this, of course, as you know, is a hammer. And this is a plane and this is a spirit-level, and this is an awl and this is a square for making right angles in wood."

She also told him to exercise great care when handling sharp-edged tools like the chisel.

She added that she was certain he would, one day, be a great craftsman like his father.

Early the following morning when the sun had risen, and when Snip-Snip had chirped from the hob, and when Banjo had played on the bicycle spokes, and when Break o' Day had crowed from the ivy bush, and when Liberator had freed himself from his stable, and when Rusty Red had bounced from his kennel, Patsy-O leaped out of bed.

He dressed himself, ate his breakfast of porridge and cream, and then made ready for the road. First he patted Rusty Red.

He said good-bye to Banjo, to Break o' Day, and to Liberator. Then he sat on his three-legged stool on the hearthstone, peeped into the crack in the hob, and said: "Good-bye to you, too, Snip-Snip."

All he could see was a green eye gleaming in

the darkness. But he felt sure that Snip-Snip was listening.

Then, with his mother's blessing on his head, and the carpenter's bast in his hand, Patsy-O set off on his journey.

Standing on a stile beside the cottage, Ita waved good-bye. At last Patsy-O was lost from sight around a bend of the twisty road.

Across the bay at the foot of the faint blue mountain lay a great town. Patsy-O had often seen its windows gleaming golden in the setting sun.

He had also seen the smoke of its hundred chimneys rising in the evening sky.

In the darkness of night he had seen its lights reflected on low clouds.

In this town he hoped to find employment.

Patsy-O walked and walked until he was quite exhausted.

He sat for a while on the grass of the roadside.

At last he was lucky enough to get a ride from an old man riding in a tub trap and driving a piebald pony. Patsy-O sat opposite him in the vehicle.

"Hup, pony!" the old man said.

The hooves of the pony moved merrily and briskly on the road.

The trap was full of packages with pictures of a steaming teapot on each package.

"I'm a tea-seller and a storyteller," said the bright-eyed man.

"Is that so?" said Patsy-O.

"Yes," said the man. "I go from farmhouse to farmhouse selling tea from the Island of Ceylon. It comes to me by ship in great chests with silver linings. I weigh the tea on small brass scales and make it up in packets of a quarter-pound, a half-pound, and a pound."

"What about the stories?" Patsy-O asked.

"I tell the children of each house stories of the giants and goblins who lived in Ireland long ago. The children love to see me coming. When I tell the children an interesting tale I stop at an exciting part. Then the children say to their mothers: 'Please, Mother, order more tea for next week so that the tea-seller will return to finish the story!' "

Then the merry-eyed man laughed heartily.

"Hup, pony!" he said in a loud voice and drove along.

For a while they were silent. Patsy-O was thinking of the Island of Ceylon and also of the giants and goblins.

"Have you ever played the Traveller's Game?" the tea-seller asked.

"No!" said Patsy-O.

"This is the way to play it. You count the animals on your side of the road and I'll count the animals on mine. The game is for a hundred points. One point for a cow, two points for a sow, four points for a horse, six points for a billy goat, eight points for a donkey with a foal, and ten points for a deer with antlers. But whoever first sees a cat asleep on a sunny window wins the game !"

Patsy-O thought this was interesting. He and the tea-seller began to play the Traveller's Game.

After some time the tea-seller had ninety-eight points and Patsy-O had scored only fifty-four points.

The boy thought he was beaten.

Suddenly on his side of the road he spied a cat asleep on a sunny window.

"Game!" he shouted at the top of his voice.

"You win," said the tea-seller with a jolly laugh.

He gave Patsy-O a packet of tea as a prize for winning the competition.

When they reached the head of the bay Patsy-O thanked the traveller and bade him good-bye.

He saw a green van with a harp on it

standing by a crossroad.

Patsy-O spoke to the driver, who was a merry postman with a brass harp on his cap. He also had a ginger moustache under his nose. He asked the postman to give him a ride to his destination.

"Hop aboard!" said the postman. "And I'll have you there in a brace of shakes."

"What's a brace of shakes?" Patsy-O wished to know.

"A brace of shakes is two shakes of a drake's tail," said the postman.

Patsy-O leaped briskly into the cab of the green van. The van was filled with mailbags.

As they rode along, the postman told Patsy-O of the wonderful picture postcards that reached him from all parts of the world, and which he delivered to the people to whom the cards were addressed.

"Where do the postcards come from?" Patsy-O asked..

"From Winnipeg and Honolulu and Constantinople and Hong Kong and Addis Ababa and Bangkok and Timbuktu. I even deliver postcards that come from Toulon and Toulouse—like a sailor's trousers."

At this the postman and Patsy-O laughed heartily together.

The time passed in pleasant chatting until at last they reached the grey walls of the town which was Patsy-O's destination.

The postman pointed out a large house with shrubs growing in brass-bound barrels in front of it.

"Ask there for lodgings," he said. "You won't be short of company. The man of the house and his wife have a baker's dozen of children."

"What's a baker's dozen?" Patsy-O wished to know.

"A baker's dozen is thirteen," shouted the jolly postman as the green van drove off.

Patsy-O was received with great kindness by the man of the house, his wife, and their thirteen children.

After supper the man of the house said to Patsy-O: "A great factory is being built in this town. If you are lucky you may find a job on the site."

Bright and early the following morning Patsy-O went to the foreman on the building site.

He told the man his name. He also said that he was a carpenter's son who had come to find work.

The foreman was a thickset man with a huge stomach.

When he looked at the small lad carrying the heavy carpenter's bast he laughed heartily.

As he did so his stomach jiggled like a plate of jelly.

"Patsy-O," he said, "you can't become a carpenter simply by wishing to be one. You must have patience. Like all carpenters, you must serve your time. First of all, I will give you the task of brewing the tea for the older carpenters. You will do this at eleven o' clock in the forenoon and again at half-past three in the afternoon. Meanwhile, if you are an intelligent lad you will keep your eyes open and master the tricks of the trade."

"What are the tricks of the trade?" Patsy-O asked.

"How to use a chisel, a plane, a hammer, an awl, and the other tools. How to join timber at the corners without using a screw or a nail."

"I see," said Patsy-O.

"When you have mastered the tricks of the trade," the foreman went on, "you will be able to make tables and chairs and stairways and partitions and banisters and many other beautiful articles of wood."

Patsy-O would have preferred to start working at the carpenter's bench at once. Yet he knew in his heart that the foreman was right.

So each day, at eleven o' clock in the forenoon and at half-past three in the afternoon, he gathered shavings and chips of wood from about the carpenters' benches.

These he placed in a large smoky container and then set them on fire.

While the fire was lighting he filled the kettle from a nearby well.

Then he turned and placed the kettle on the flames. When the water was boiling he brewed the tea.

At first he used the package of tea the old tea-seller had given him as a prize. The carpenters said it was the finest tea they had ever tasted. They became very friendly with Patsy-O.

So the days passed.

All the time Patsy-O kept his eyes open and watched what the older carpenters were doing. Thus he picked up the tricks of the trade.

He learned how to saw wood, how to make it smooth, and how to join it at the corners without using a screw or a nail.

He also learned the names of different woods. Presently he could tell beech from oak and oak from ash and ash from pine.

He also learned about mahogany which is used for furniture and teak which is used for shop fronts and for shipbuilding.

After some weeks the foreman said to Patsy-O:

"I've been watching you carefully and I think you are an intelligent lad.

I think you have learned enough to start as a carpenter's help. Tomorrow I'll put another lad brewing the tea. You will stand at the carpenter's bench and work like the older men."

From this onward, Patsy-O began to earn good money. This he hid safely in a leather belt around his waist.

Everybody praised the boy and said he would be as good a carpenter as his father.

Every Sunday afternoon without fail, if the weather was fine, Patsy-O climbed up the winding pathway to the mountain peak above the town.

If the day was very clear he could look across the bay and spy on the other side the white speck that was his mother's cottage.

So the days passed.

Red summer changed into yellow autumn. Yellow autumn changed into silver winter.

The great factory began to take shape. The townspeople came out to wonder at its size and at the splendid workmanship of the men who had built it.

By now Patsy-O had quite a large sum of money saved up in his belt.

Everyone working on the huge building— the carpenters, the stonemasons, the electricians, the plasterers, the plumbers, and the fitters—all knew of Patsy-O's plans.

They helped and encouraged him as much as they could.

Very early on the day before Christmas Eve, Patsy-O said farewell to the kind foreman and to his fellow tradesmen.

He also said goodbye to the father and mother and to the baker's dozen of children who lived in the house where he had lodged.

Proudly carrying his bast of tools, he turned his face towards the east. He had the idea of travelling to the head of the bay, then making his way westward along the shore until he had reached his home.

He hoped that on the way he might get a bed for the night from some kindly person in a wayside cottage.

The work in the open air had made Patsy-O quite strong. The carpenter's bast was not now a great load.

He walked gaily along the roadway that ran by the edge of the sea.

He laughed with joy to see the sea-gulls high in the sky.

He laughed with joy to see a fisherman's black boat bounding on the sea.

He laughed with joy to see little waves like white horses racing in the ocean.

He laughed too as he thought how he would surprise and delight his mother and his sister Ita. And as he thought of his five faithful pets, he sang a merry song.

He walked along until nightfall.

All he met was an old nanny-goat with a grey and white beard and two long horns who looked at him quite peevishly and said: "Meggy-meg-meg, don't touch my leg or I'll puck you with my horn-ie-o."

At least that's what Patsy-O thought the old nanny-goat was saying. And if he wasn't sure of this, he was quite sure that the nanny was telling him that it was rude to stare and that he had best be off with himself wherever he was going.

Night was drawing near. The air grew quite cold. There was a glare of snow on the mountaintops. The stars were glittering in the sky.

By now, he was quite tired after his day's travelling. He trudged along the twisting, winding, wandering road.

Darkness descended on the world. After a while a full moon looked down on the boy. "Oh, dear! Oh, dear!" said Patsy-O.

Just then he spied a light in a cottage window. The cottage stood on the edge of a tall cliff above the sea.

Patsy-O knocked on the door.

After a while a little old woman came out. She had comical spectacles on her buttony nose.

"Tut-tut-tut and pepoo!" said the old woman quite crossly indeed. "What is it you want? Who are you? Where are you from?"

These quick questions took Patsy-O somewhat aback. However, he told the old woman of his plight.

He also told her that he wished to be home for Christmas to light the tall white candle on the kitchen windowsill.

The woman said—again quite crossly— "Tut-tut-tut and pepoo! Come in! I shall give you something to eat. But you musn't stay! You must be off before they come back! You understand?"

Patsy-O didn't at all understand. But he pretended that he did.

He was glad to get in out of the cold air. The turf fire blazing on the hearth and the stool beside it made him think of his home.

"Tut-tut-tut! " said the old lady—and this time she forgot to add "pepoo"—"Sit on the stool! Warm yourself! I will give you something to eat! Then you must be off!"

A great pile of wool was drying in front of the fire.

"Pepoo!" the little woman snapped—and this time she forgot to say "tut-tut-tut"— "Keep your wits about you! Eat quickly! See that the wool doesn't catch fire!"

Patsy-O was thankful to be allowed to set down his load and to sit on the stool in the chimney corner.

He was glad too to take the blue mug of milk and the triangle of yellow meal bread with golden butter on it that the old woman gave him.

He thanked her kindly for the meal.

Patsy-O was as hungry as a ploughman. He was as thirsty as a traveller in the desert. He was as tired as a hunting dog at the end of a day's chase.

He began to eat the bread and butter and to drink the milk.

Meanwhile, the old woman set four blue mugs and four blue platters on the table. They were the largest mugs and the largest platters Patsy-O had ever seen.

From time to time the old woman glanced out the window. She was looking over the sea as if expecting to see a boat approaching the shore.

Now and again, too, she lifted the cover of a big cauldron hanging from a hook above the fire.

As she did so the smell of stew filled the kitchen.

The delicious smell made Patsy-O hungrier than ever.

"Hurry up!" the woman snapped—and this time she forgot both the "tut-tut-tut" and the "pepoo".

Patsy-O did his best to hurry and eat the meal she had given him.

But he had travelled so far that he grew drowsy with the heat of the fire.

Even before he had finished the meal, his head fell on his breast and his eyes closed in sleep.

The old woman was so busy that she did not

notice him. Either that or she was short-sighted.

Just then, the fire melted the last knob of butter on Patsy-O's bread. The melted butter fell upon a piece of curled wool at his feet. This happened as the old woman had opened the door and was looking out.

A breeze from the sea blew through the kitchen. It rolled the buttery curl of wool into the fire.

The curl immediately sprang up in flames.

Then, as again the old woman slammed the door, a breeze blew down the chimney. The blazing curl was blown right out of the fire. It fell on the wool and set the bale on fire.

The old woman straightened her comical glasses on her buttony nose. She began to sniff loudly.

Spying the wool ablaze, she began to cry out in a loud voice.

The smell of burning wool, the crackling of the flames, and the screeching of the old woman woke Patsy-O.

He was lucky to escape from the chimney corner with only his clothes scorched and his hair singed.

He grabbed the bast and raced for the door.

The old woman raced after him roaring as

loudly as she could.

Patsy-O ran straight into the arms of four burly men, each of whom carried a huge cask upon his shoulder.

The biggest man of the four dropped his barrel and grabbed the boy.

Patsy-O then realized that he had come into a nest of smugglers—a father and three great sons who smuggled liquor into Ireland from the low Lowlands of Holland.

He trembled with fear.

The men stood by furiously as they watched their cottage burn. So fierce was the blaze that they could do nothing to quench it.

At last the roof fell down in a million sparks. The smugglers were so angry that they seemed ready to tear Patsy-O to pieces.

"Let us kill him at once," the father growled.

The sons, too, growled their agreement.

The old woman pleaded for a chance for the boy.

"Tut-tut-tut and pepoo!" she said. "He meant no harm. Besides, he seems to be a hardworking little chap."

"What shall we do if he tells the Civic Guards?" said the father of the smugglers.

"Or the Revenue Men?" said the eldest of the sons.

"If he does that we shall all end our days in prison," said the second son.

"Never again shall we be able to smuggle liquor from the low Lowlands of Holland!" said the third son.

After much argument the smugglers decided to place Patsy-O in a hogshead, to batten down the head of it and throw the cask into the ocean.

The hogshead would float out into the middle of the sea and no trace of the boy would ever again be found.

One of the sons suggested that the carpenter's bast should be placed in a smaller tierce and that it, too, should be cast into the sea.

Then there would be no clues for the Civic Guards or the Revenue Men if they came nosing about.

To this all agreed.

The smugglers placed Patsy-O in the empty hogshead. Setting the head on it, they fastened it with battens and nails.

Placing the bast of tools in the smaller tierce, they did likewise.

With a mighty heave they sent the larger barrel rolling down the green grassy slope that led to the cliff edge.

Striking an anthill, it leaped high into the air. The hogshead fell with a splash into the green ocean.

The cask landed upside down. At first Patsy-O found himself standing on his head. After much kicking and pushing he managed to right the barrel.

Just then he heard a smaller splash a little distance away from him.

Then he knew that the tierce containing the carpenter's tools had also been thrown into the sea.

Outside the barrel the sea roared like a lion.

Again and again, Patsy-O felt himself being borne high on the crest of a great billow and then falling into the deep trough between two waves.

Sometimes the little tierce butted against the bigger hogshead as if to say, "I am still here, Patsy-O! Do not lose courage! Somehow we shall all escape!"

Then a huge wave that was just receding from the cliff took both the barrels out to sea.

Patsy-O began to lose hope. He felt that he was drifting farther and farther away from the Irish shore.

Only the knock-knock of the tierce against his own hogshead gave him some comfort.

Away, away, Patsy-O drifted.

At last the boy remembered something he had heard a cooper say to one of the carpenters on the building site.

His fingers began to search around inside the staves of the hogshead. After much fumbling he found the bung of the barrel.

He doubled up his fist and began striking at the circular piece of wood. At last he heard a tiny squeak. He knew then that the bung was moving. With a strong blow he fisted the bung into the sea.

Now there was a circular hole about four or five inches in diameter through which he could look out upon the water.

The first thing he saw was the tierce bobbing a short distance away. Night passed. Dawn came like a fire lighted behind the peaks of Kerry.

Porpoises played beside the barrel, diving and dodging quite close to him like wheels of shining skin.

Now and again a gannet high in the air spied a fish in the sea below. Descending at a great speed, the bird struck the water with a splash. Then it came up with a green and blue mackerel wriggling in its beak.

Now and again a school of puffins bobbed up

beside the hogshead. They looked cheekily at the eye of Patsy-O which they could see plainly in the bunghole of the floating barrel.

"Oh, dear! Oh, dear!" said Patsy-O. He knew that neither the fishes nor the birds could help him to escape.

About noon, a Spanish trawler passed by.

"Help! Help!" the boy yelled loudly.

The fishermen were too busy shooting their trawls into the sea. They did not hear Patsy-O's cries for aid.

They laughed at the sight of the floating barrel and said that it was surely empty.

It was now Christmas Eve, the day on which Patsy-O had promised his mother that he would return to light the tall candle.

By mid-afternoon Patsy-O realized that the hills of his native land did not seem quite so far away as they had been in the morning.

He now began to hope that the turning tide would bear him back towards his own land.

This is exactly what happened.

As the tide turned, the hogshead floated nearer and nearer to the shore.

At last, with great joy in his heart, Patsy-O recognized the mountain above his home.

The sun was setting in the west. By its golden light, Patsy-O saw his own cottage nestling above the beach.

He could even see the white unlighted candle on the windowsill inside.

Then he saw the kitchen lamp spring into flame. He could barely see his mother's face behind the four panes of the small window.

Ita was standing close beside her.

Although it was too far away to be sure, Patsy-O thought that their faces were melancholy.

Darkness came down over the bay. The sea had grown calm. The moon lighted up the sky.

The barrel floated about a half a mile from the shore.

At last Patsy-O thought of a plan.

He put the first two fingers of his right hand and the first two fingers of his left hand into his mouth. He placed the tips of the two middle fingers close together, but at an angle.

He pressed the tip of his tongue against his fingertips.

Placing his mouth as close to the bunghole as he could, he whistled through his fingers.

Again and again he whistled with all his might.

The cat was asleep on the hearth. The cock was asleep in the bush. The donkey was asleep in the stable.

As for Rusty Red, he was high on the mountainside hunting a fox.

Snip-Snip, however, was wide awake. The cricket had keen ears. Although the whistle came from far away, the little insect heard it plainly.

Snip-Snip come out of the crack behind the hob. His green eyes glistened. The whistle was so faint that neither Patsy-O's mother nor Ita could hear it.

Snip-Snip rubbed his wings together as strongly as he could but he was so small that no one took any notice. Suddenly he jumped right into the cat's ear and snip-snipped for dear life.

Of course, this woke Banjo. The cat cocked his other ear. He too heard the faint whistle from the sea.

Banjo miaowed. But he was unable to miaow very loudly. No one took any notice of Banjo.

The cat then raced into the little pantry where the bicycle stood.

Stretching out a long paw he twanged loudly on the spokes. Then Banjo leaped up to the small open window of the pantry. From there he jumped onto the roof of the carpenter's workshop.

The music of the spokes roused Break o' Day from his roost in the ivy bush.

The cock heard Pasty-O whistling. He began to crow as loudly as he could.

Liberator, too, woke up.

"This was the shortest night I can ever remember," he said grumpily and set about freeing himself.

As he stumbled out into the darkness he too heard the whistle from the sea. The donkey began to bray for all he was worth.

Immediately Banjo, with Snip-Snip still in his ear, leaped down from the workshop roof onto the donkey's broad back.

Break o' Day fluttered down from the ivy bush to perch between the donkey's ears.

All four looked up at the mountainside.

Liberator gave a tremendous hee-haw. The cat miaowed. The cricket snipped. The cock crew loudly.

On the mountainside, hot on the trail of a fox, Rusty Red pricked up his ears. He heard the noise from below.

He listened very carefully.

Just then, he too heard the whistle from the sea.

He knew the whistle was his master's.

Rusty Red came bounding down to where

his companions were waiting in the tiny paddock beside the cottage.

The red setter cleared the stone wall with a single bound.

Barking loudly he rushed out the little wicket gate that led to the beach.

He was followed by Liberator with Break o' Day on his head and Banjo clinging to his back for dear life. And of course Snip-Snip was still inside the cat's ear.

The faithful friends raced towards the beach. At the tide-lip they halted.

Then all the other pets together looked down at Rusty Red.

The brave dog understood at once.

He sprang into the waves and swam in the direction from which the whistle came.

Rusty Red swam and swam.

At last he reached the barrel. Still swimming, he put his muzzle through the hole—for that is all that would fit–and began to lick his master's face.

The brave dog then tried to push the barrel with his paws in an effort to get it ashore. But he was in danger of upsetting the hogshead and of sending the water flooding through he bunghole.

Patsy-O told him to stop pushing.

Not knowing how to save his master, the faithful dog was now frantic.

He swam splashingly all around the hogshead.

Patsy-O then remembered the merry times when he had played with Rusty Red on the snowy mountainside and in the summer sea.

Putting his mouth close to the bunghole he shouted: "Turn your brush, Rusty Red, turn your brush!"

The intelligent dog understood at once.

He turned right about in the water.

The tip of his tail brushed against the bunghole of the barrel.

Patsy-O put out his thumb and forefinger as far as he could. He tried to catch the dog's tail.

At first he failed.

Then he caught a rib of red hair, then a lock of red hair, and then a curl of red hair.

At last he caught the tail itself and drew it into the barrel.

Gently but firmly, his two hands gripped the setter's tail.

Then he shouted for all he was worth: "Hie for home, Rusty Red! Rusty Red, hie for home!"

The setter began to swim towards the shore

with great strokes of his powerful legs.

Presently they reached shallow water. Rusty Red dragged the barrel right up onto the dry beach.

Patsy-O released the dog's tail.

Hearing all the commotion and hullabaloo, Patsy-O's mother rushed down to the beach.

Ita came running too.

"In heaven's name, what is it?" the widow asked in alarm.

"It's only me, Mother," said Patsy-O from the barrel.

"Goodness, gracious, mercy!" said Patsy-O's mother.

Just then the little tierce came floating in on the ripples of the sea.

"Break open the head of the smaller barrel with a stone," Patsy-O told his mother, "and you'll find the tools to release me."

The widow did as her son asked.

She stove in the head of the tierce with a blow of a stone. Then she took out the tools.

Before you could say, "Chopsticks," Patsy-O was standing on the beach with his mother's arms around him and the five pets leaping with delight.

All returned to the cottage.

"Mother!" said Patsy-O. "I have money in a

leather belt around my waist. I shall buy all sorts of good things for you and Ita. And of course, I won't forget to buy something for each of my five wonderful pets."

"The head of a herring for Banjo," Patsy-O said. "Some oats for Break o' Day. A mash of bran for Liberator. And a large juicy ox bone for Rusty Red."

Just then Snip-Snip jumped out of the cat's ear and vanished into the crack in the wall. As he did so Patsy-O saw the little insect for the first time.

"I don't know what present to give you, Snip-Snip," he said, "but I promise always to keep a bright fire on the hearth so that your wings will never grow cold."

Then Patsy-O put the wicker panniers on Liberator's brown back.

Together they went off to the store.

Presently, they returned with a turkey and a ham and a plum pudding and multicoloured jellies.

They also brought Christmas crackers and paper chains and garlands for the kitchen.

Patsy-O did not forget to fetch the gifts he had promised the pets.

As he came down the mountain road he plucked some holly with red knobs on it and some green laurel as well.

Finally, he took one small branch of ivy from the bush in which Break o' Day spent his nights.

"When the kitchen is decorated with paper chains and garlands and evergreens," he said, "it will be lovely."

When the cottage kitchen was decorated with paper chains and garlands and evergreens, Ita clapped her hands with joy.

Then Patsy-O lighted the tall Christmas candle on the windowsill. The pets looked on in wonder.

Then all, except Snip-Snip of course, who didn't really need it, had an appetizing meal.

"Time for sleep now," said Patsy-O's mother to the pets.

The pets went off to their sleeping places. All except Snip-Snip who was already in his sleeping place.

Patsy-O then sat on his three-legged stool and told his mother and Ita of his adventures.

When he told her how well he succeeded at the carpentry his mother was quite proud.

"When the New Year is come and as each day grows longer by a cock's step," she said, "you may open the workshop again. Then you may begin to make beautiful articles of wood just as your father did in days of old."

This made Patsy-O very happy.

By and by he felt sleepy. Ita had already gone to bed.

At last, still sitting on the three-legged stool, Patsy-O's head dropped on his breast. Before very long he was fast asleep.

His mother lifted him gently and laid him on his warm bed. She tucked the bedclothes in about him and drew the bedroom door to without making a sound.

Patsy-O's mother then walked to the half-door and looked out at the stable. The door was closed and Liberator was fast asleep.

She looked at the kennel. She saw the sleeping head of Rusty Red resting on his two front paws.

She looked at the ivy bush. Head under his wing, Break o' Day was in the land of dreams.

She looked at the flag of the hearth. Stretched out before the fire, Banjo was slumbering.

She looked at the back of the hob. Not a sound from Snip-Snip.

Softly, she closed the door of the cottage. In the middle of the kitchen she stood and listened.

The children too were breathing gently in

sleep.

Then the widow began to smile with joy.

Once again the little cottage was filled with peace.

As for the cruel smugglers who had placed Patsy-O in the hogshead, they were captured by the Civic Guards who had gone to investigate the burning cottage.

Be that as it may, Patsy-O's mother and sister and Patsy-O himself of course and his five wonderful pets were now as happy and as happy and as happy and as happy and as happy as the lovely days are

L   O   N   G

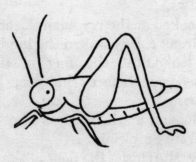

Patsy-O Goes to Spain

Patsy-O Goes to Spain

atsy-O came running into the cottage kitchen.

"Have you seen Rusty Red?" he asked his mother who was a widow.

"I have not seen your Irish setter since morning," his mother answered.

"Have *you* seen Rusty Red?" Patsy-O asked his sister Ita.

"No!" replied Ita.

"What shall I do?" Patsy-O said with a sigh. He went to the window and looked out at the sea in front of their cottage home. "I have whistled for my dog on the hillside," he said. "I have called his name among the trees. I have shouted for him on the beach. But alas, Rusty Red is nowhere to be found."

The boy knelt on the hearth and peeped into a crack in the wall behind the fireplace.

"Have *you* seen Rusty Red?" he asked the

second of his pets—a cricket called Snip-Snip.

"Snip-snip," said the cricket. Patsy-O knew by the special way the cricket made the sound that he had not seen the dog.

Patsy-O rushed out to the donkey's stable.

"Have *you* seen Rusty Red?" he asked Liberator the Donkey.

"Hee-haw," said Liberator the Donkey. Patsy-O knew by the special way the donkey brayed that he too had not seen the missing dog.

Patsy-O looked up at the ivy bush which grew near the cottage.

"Have *you* seen Rusty Red?" he called out to Break o' Day, his black and gold cock.

"Cock-a-doodle-doo," Break o' Day called out rather grumpily. He was grumpy because he liked to crow only when day was breaking. And it was afternoon now.

Of course this also meant that the cock had not seen the Irish setter.

"And you?" Patsy-O asked Banjo the marmalade-coloured cat who was asleep on the sunny wall above the little cove. "Have *you* seen Rusty Red?"

"Mee-ah-ow!" Banjo said opening his eyes. Then stretching out a claw he plucked the spokes of a bicycle lying against the wall. The sound Banjo made was as if someone had begun to play a banjo.

None of Patsy-O's pets had seen the red setter.

"Have you searched for him on the pier?" the boy's mother asked.

"No, mother," Patsy-O said.

"Rusty Red likes to visit the pier and watch the fishing boats come and go," Ita said.

"I shall go to the pier then," Patsy-O said. He rushed off to the pier as fast as his legs could carry him.

* * * *

On the way he looked across the fence into a field. Old Mother Moloney's black Kerry cow was eating grass. The cow had one straight horn and one curly one.

She was a cross-patch cow. She glared at Patsy-O as he hurried by. She did not like Patsy-O or his dog Rusty Red.

One day in summer Patsy-O was picking mushrooms in the field. He had almost filled his white gallon with mushrooms when the cow came rushing up behind him.

"Moooo," she said loudly. This meant "Get out of my field at once!" The cow did not eat mushrooms so this was most unmannerly of her. Patsy-O took to his heels. The angry cow came running close behind him.

Just then Rusty Red had come rushing up. "Catch her brush, Rusty-Red!" Patsy-O shouted to his faithful dog.

The red setter leaped for the cow's tail, gripped it firmly between his teeth and hung on for dear life.

The cow came to a stop. As she drew back her leg to kick Rusty Red the dog let go his grip. By this time Patsy-O was safely over the gate. Rusty Red came scampering behind him. The red setter was barking with joy.

Ever since that day the Kerry cow and Rusty Red weren't friends. Now the cow glared at the boy as if to say, "So your red setter is not with you today. I hope that he is lost! Serve him right!"

* * * *

Patsy-O walked along the edge of the pier. He looked down on the decks of the fishing trawlers. Boxes of fish swung over his head. The boxes were being loaded onto lorries. Nets were spread out to dry on the sea wall. He asked the fishermen if they had seen his dog.

All shook their heads.

Old Salt sat on a fish-box by the pier wall. He had sailed the Seven Seas. He had been shipwrecked seven times. His eyes were closed. It seemed that the old sailor was having forty winks.

As Patsy-O passed by, Old Salt opened one eye and said—

Patsy-O is full of sorrow
For Rusty Red won't be home tomorrow.

"Do you know where he is?" Patsy-O asked Old Salt.

Eena meena mina mo,
Of course, of course, of course, I know,

said Old Salt.

"Please tell me where I can find him," Patsy-O said.

He's gone to a land where there's no rain
Your red red dog has gone off to Spain.

"To Spain?" Patsy-O echoed in surprise.

On a Spanish trawler he fell asleep
And now he's far on the briny deep,

muttered Old Salt.

"You mean that Rusty Red has gone off to Spain on a Spanish trawler?" Patsy-O asked the old seaman.

But Old Salt's head had fallen on his breast. Bending down to catch what he was saying, Patsy-O could barely hear:

Another trawler sails at dawn
Follow the track your dog has gone.

With that the old poet-sailor began to snore loudly.

"There must be another Spanish trawler here," said Patsy-O to himself. He raced along the pier. Just then he saw a beautiful trawler. It had the figurehead of a saint painted blue and gold.

The name on its prow was San Antonio which means Saint Anthony. The boy spoke to the Captain.

"Please, Captain," Patsy-O said, "take me with you to the sunny land of Spain."

"Slow! Slow! señor," said the Captain whose name was Pedro. "Why a boy like you wish to go to sunny Spain, eh?"

"My Irish setter fell asleep on board a Spanish trawler this morning. The trawler sailed off. Please take me to Spain so that I may find my dog and bring him back," the boy pleaded.

"Si, si, señor, I take you," Captain Pedro

said, "but first you must get permission from your father and the schoolmaster."

"My father is dead!" Patsy-O said sadly. "But I'm sure that my mother will give me leave to go."

"Ask the schoolmaster too!" said Captain Pedro as the boy raced off.

Patsy-O rushed home. "Please mother, may I go to sunny Spain?" he asked.

"Goodness, gracious, mercy!" his mother said. "Spain is a thousand miles from here."

"But if I do not follow Rusty Red I shall never lay eyes on him again."

"Very well. You may go. But do be careful!" the boy's mother said with a sigh. "And be sure to return as soon as ever you can."

"I shall be back in Ireland to walk in the procession on St Patrick's Day," Patsy-O said with a brave smile. "I shall wear the harp and shamrock on my jacket and Rusty Red will be walking by my side."

The following morning Patsy-O was up at the crack of dawn. He put on his white Aran sweater. On his head he placed a white woollen cap with pom-poms on it. He carried some knick-knacks in a bundle.

After his breakfast he was ready to go.

"Snip-snip!" chirped his cricket by way of

good-bye.

"Hee-haw!" brayed Liberator the Donkey.

"Cock-a-doodle-doo!" called Break o' Day.

"Mee-ah-ow!" said Banjo the Cat.

"Goodbye!" said Ita. Her voice was sad.

"Goodbye, my brave son!" said Patsy-O's mother.

Ita and her mother waved goodbye until Patsy-O was out of sight round a bend in the road.

Patsy-O soon came to the school. It stood at the top of a sloping wall of small grey stones. The children were in the playground.

When the boys and girls saw Patsy-O coming they stood in a row at the wall and looked down at him. The children looked like a row of apples on a high shelf.

"Where are you off to, Patsy-O?' they asked.

"To sunny Spain!"

"To Spain?" the children echoed with one voice.

The schoolmaster, Master O'Hay, came to the wall and looked down. He was bald and wore spectacles on his nose. As he peeped over the wall his head looked more like an egg than an apple.

"Please, Master O'Hay," Patsy-O piped, "may I go to Spain to find my Irish setter?"

"Homm, Hamm, Humm!" said the schoolmaster. "What is the capital of Spain?"

"Madrid!" said Patsy-O.

"On what river does Madrid stand?"

"On the river Tagus."

"Who discovered America?"

"In fourteen hundred and ninety-two, Columbus crossed the ocean blue," said Patsy-O.

"Right three times," said the schoolmaster. "Off you pop to sunny Spain! But don't forget! Be back again for St Patrick's Day."

"Go raibh maith agat, a Mháistir," Patsy-O said thanking the schoolmaster in Irish.

When he reached the pier he hopped aboard the Spanish trawler.

Seated on the fish-box Old Salt was still sound asleep. The trawler put out to sea. Soon the blue mountains of Kerry were out of sight. The vessel sailed southward for Spain.

Pedro, the Captain came along. He had a deck-scrub in his hand.

"You must work your passage, Patsy-O," he said with a smile.

"What does that mean?" the boy wanted to know.

"You must do jobs instead of paying your fare."

"I shall be glad to work my passage!" Patsy-O said. He took the deck-scrub. He then poured water on the deck and began to brush the fish scales off the white boards.

"Very good!" said Captain Pedro when he returned.

The crew were very kind to Patsy-O. They pointed out sea-birds such as puffins and cormorants. They showed him the whiskery head of a seal swimming close to the trawler. Then they put their nets in the open sea.

When the nets were drawn, the deck was a mass of fish—cod and hake and herring and mackerel and plaice and sole. There was also a large sting ray with wings like a bird.

Patsy-O had never seen so many fish together before.

All the fish he had caught up to this was one small trout with red spots on its scales.

He had also caught stickleback which he kept in a jam jar.

"Shall I see flying fish?" Patsy-O asked.

"Not in these latitudes!" one of the crew said. "Flying fish appear nearer the Equator. There the water is warmer."

"We must keep a sharp look out for large vessels," the Captain said. "We are now sailing across the Atlantic sea-lanes."

That evening at dusk a great liner passed by. To Patsy-O it seemed like a lighted city. He could see passengers walking up and down on the deck. Some of them stood at the rail and waved to the trawler; Patsy-O waved his cap with the pom-poms on it. The passengers laughed when they saw the boy in the trawler.

The following day Captain Pedro looked up at the sky. He switched on the radio and listened carefully. "We often have a storm in the Bay of Biscay," Captain Pedro said to the boy. "So be prepared, Patsy-O."

Soon the storm broke. The trawler was tossed about like a cork on the angry waves. The wind howled and whistled. The Irish boy was frightened out of his wits. But Captain Pedro laughed softly. "Have no fear, Patsy-O," he said. "The storm will soon pass."

The Captain was right. As they drew nearer to Spain the sea became calm. That evening the boy looked about him in wonder. They were entering a harbour crowded with shipping.

The Captain blew three short blasts and a long one on the trawler's hooter. "Hoh hoh hoh, hooo"—just like that.

"My señora and family know I come home," he said. He pointed at a house on the hillside above the bay.

From the lawn in front of the house someone waved a white shawl; Captain Pedro waved back. Patsy waved his woollen cap with the pom-poms on it.

The town was decorated with flags and bunting. A band was playing in the square in front of the Cathedral. "Rat-a-tat," said the drums. "Bop-a-bop-a-o," said the trumpets. "Oppa-oppa-op-pap-pa," said the sliding trombones.

"Tomorrow is the fiesta of San Pedro," said Captain Pedro.

"What is a fiesta?" Patsy-O said.

"It is a feast day or a holiday," Pedro said— "just like you have on St Patrick's Day in Ireland. Tomorrow we honour San Pedro or Saint Peter. The fiesta lasts for several days."

As the Captain stepped on to the pier his wife Dolores and his children—Andrea a girl, and Pedrito a boy about Patsy-O's age— came rushing towards him. The Captain opened his arms and gave all three a great hug of love.

"Who is this fine boy?" the Captain's wife asked.

"This is Patsy-O from Ireland," Pedro said. "His Irish setter came here to Spain by mistake on board a trawler. Take him home with you," he told the children, "and make him welcome. Your mother and I shall return to eat supper with you. But first I must sell my fish and pay off my crew."

Captain Pedro and his wife went off together.

Andrea took Patsy-O by the right hand and Pedrito took the boy by the left hand. The three children walked through the town. They skipped uphill along the narrow road that led to their home. The night air was warm.

When they reached the house they showed Patsy-O into a beautiful bedroom. From the balcony of his room he could look down on the town and the harbour.

Suddenly Patsy-O remembered something he had heard a Spanish sailor say. "Gracias, amigos," he said which means "Thanks, friends".

Andrea and Pedrito clapped their hands with joy.

Just then Captain Pedro and his wife Dolores returned. "You have brought me luck," Captain Pedro told Patsy-O. "I've got a big price for my fish. We also have good news for you," he added. "Your dog, Rusty Red, has been in this town. But he runs off when anyone tries to catch him. He cannot be far away."

The children's mother prepared a lovely meal of paella. As darkness fell they ate supper on a table on the balcony. A fireworks display was being held in the town. Rockets rushed up into the sky.

"Who-o-o-issh" the rockets said. Then they burst into thousands of pink, yellow, purple and sky-blue stars. The children were delighted.

In the town too bands were playing. Soldiers marched up and down. Dancers moved in and out in the square. Clack-clack went the castanets. The sound of music and laughter floated up to them.

"You are sleepy, Patsy-O," the Captain said when the meal ended. "We have much to do tomorrow." Patsy-O went off to bed.

As soon as his head touched the pillow he was sound asleep.

When he awoke in the morning he found the sunlight streaming into the room. At first he thought that he was at home in his own cottage by the sea in Ireland with his mother and his sister, Ita.

He cocked his ear to hear Break o' Day saying "Hurrah, hurrah it's break of day" or to hear Liberator braying "Hee-haw, hee-haw."

or Snip-Snip, the cricket saying "Snip-snip" or
Banjo the Cat twanging on the bicycle spokes
or Rusty Red barking for someone to throw a
stick into the sea so that he could plunge in
and bring it back.

Then the boy remembered where he was. He
was in the sunny land of Spain! He washed
himself, put on his sweater and knitted cap
and pulled on a pair of sandals.

After breakfast the family went to the
Cathedral of San Pedro. As they walked along,
Patsy-O's eyes were looking out for Rusty Red.
Alas, the setter was nowhere to be seen.

On the walls were huge posters. These told
that a bullfight would take place later that
afternoon.

After church, the Mayor of the town spoke to
Captain Pedro: "I have heard about the Irish
boy and his lost dog," he said.

"Bring him and your children along to my
special box at the bullfight this afternoon."

"Gracias, señor," Captain Pedro said with a
bow.

After the midday meal the children's
mother said, "Now we have our siesta".

"A siesta?" Patsy-O said. "Is it a kind of
fiesta?"

Captain Pedro laughed and said. "Oh no! It

means that we shall all go to sleep."

"But it is still daytime," said Patsy-O.

"In hot countries like Spain we rest in the early afternoon." Dolores said, "Off to bed now. We shall get up when the heat of the day has passed."

Patsy-O thought it odd of everyone to go to sleep at such a time. But he did as the others did. Some hours later he awoke. He felt very refreshed.

Then Captain Pedro and Pedrito and Patsy-O went off to the bullfight. They rode in the Captain's old boneshaker.

The children's mother said she did not like to watch bullfighting. "It is a dangerous sport," she said. "Many of the bullfighters are wounded. Some are even killed." So she and Andrea stayed at home. Were it not for his dog, Patsy-O too would have remained at home.

Crowds of people were going to the Corrida or bullfight.

The Captain honked his horn loudly as he drove along. Hens and chickens flew in all directions. Dogs barked loudly at the old jalopy.

When they reached the plaza or bullring they went into the Mayor's special box. This was on the shady side of the arena. The Mayor welcomed them.

The place was crowded. Merry music set the crowds laughing.

The Mayor made a speech. Trumpets blew. The bullfighters began to parade.

Each bullfighter was dressed in a beautiful suit. The suit twinkled as if it was covered with stars. "It is called 'the suit of lights,' " Captain Pedro told Patsy-O. "Do you see that man in front? He is the most famous matador or bullfighter in the whole of Spain."

Everyone cheered when the parade ended.

Again a trumpet blew! The gate of the bull-pen flew open. A great black bull came bounding into the ring. His white horns flashed in the sunlight. He bellowed and pawed the sand.

The famous bullfighter went out to fight the fierce animal.

He took with him a red cape on a stick. When the bull saw the red cape he lowered his head and charged with all his might. But as the bull came near the matador drew the cape across his own body.

The bull's horns passed through the cape. The horns did not touch the bullfighter.

The crowd were very excited. "Olé!" they

cried.

Again and again the bull rushed at the matador. Again and again the cruel horns passed harmlessly through the cape. The bull was now very angry. "Toro!" the bullfighter called again.

As the bull charged, the matador turned too quickly. He slipped onto the sand and fell to his knees. Before he could rise to his feet again the bull struck him with his cruel horns. He tossed the matador into the air.

A groan of horror rose from the crowd. The most famous matador in all Spain was in danger of being killed!

The wounded matador staggered to his feet. The bull turned. He lowered his head. He struck the sand with his hooves. He bellowed loudly and prepared to charge.

The bull thundered forward. The crowd held its breath.

Just then, moving like a flash, a red setter dog raced through the open gateway of the bull-pen. The dog was Rusty-Red.

Patsy-O came to his feet at once.

Cupping his hands about his mouth the boy shouted "Catch his brush, Rusty Red! Rusty Red, catch his brush!"

The brave dog heard his master's voice. Just

as the sharp horns were about to pierce the breast of the matador the Irish setter leaped. He aimed at the tuft of hair at the end of the bull's tail. He gripped it with his strong white teeth. The bull stopped just in the nick of time.

The bull tried to shake off the dog but Rusty Red hung on for dear life. Just as he had once hung on to the tail of Mother Moloney's cow!

The crowd roared with relief and joy. "Olé!" they shouted. A man rushed into the ring. He helped the wounded matador to safety.

The bull trotted twice around the ring with Rusty Red hanging on to his tail. "Olé!" the crowd roared. Everybody was laughing.

Then the fierce beast headed for the open gateway. Just before he went out, Patsy-O whistled and Rusty Red let go his grip. The brave dog trotted over to the space in front of the Mayor's box. There he sat down, wagged his tail and barked joyfully up at his master.

"Come, Rusty Red!" Patsy-O called. He spread his arms wide.

The setter sprang over the barrier. He leaped right into Patsy-O's arms and began to lick his master's face.

"Olé," the crowd roared.

The Mayor took Patsy-O by the hand. He led him out into the ring. Rusty Red followed. The

Mayor, his hat held high, led the boy and the dog around the ring.

Everyone was clapping hands and cheering. Girls took flowers out of their hair and flung them down before them. Rich men threw their purses into the ring. The purses were full of money.

A huge matador, brother of the injured bullfighter came along. His name was Maxim. He lifted Patsy-O onto his shoulders. The boy clung to Maxim's head. Patsy-O waved to everyone, most of all to his friends, Captain Pedro and Pedrito.

It was the happiest bullfight ever held in the sunny land of Spain.

That night Rusty Red slept beside Patsy-O on a mat on the bedroom floor. When Patsy-O opened his eyes in the morning. he remembered that St Patrick's Day was drawing near.

He also remembered his promise to his mother and his sister, Ita. He had said that he would be home for St Patrick's Day and that he would pin the shamrock and the green harp with the gold strings on his jacket. And that Rusty Red would walk beside him in the parade.

Captain Pedro came into the room. He was

wearing his yellow oilskins over his thigh boots.

"The fiesta is ended, my young friend," he said. "Today we return to the Atlantic fishing grounds."

Patsy-O was glad to hear this. It meant that he was returning to his mother, his sister and his other pets in Ireland. He looked down at his red dog and said. "We shall hie for home, Rusty Red."

The clever setter wagged his tail to show that he understood.

The Irish lad thanked the Captain's wife for her kindness. He then bade her goodbye. With Rusty Red at his heels and Captain Pedro, Andrea and Pedrito beside him, he made his way down to the harbour.

Most of the people they met had been to the bullfight. They patted Rusty Red on the head and shook hands with Patsy-O.

"You are a brave boy and this is a brave dog!" they said.

On the roadside three boys were playing a strange game. One was pretending to be a bull. He was using two fingers as horns. One of the other boys had a red handkerchief which he pretended was a bullfighter's cape. The "bull" pushed the "matador" to the ground by nudging him with his head.

The third boy leaped out from behind a rock. He growled like a dog and rushing forward caught the "bull" by the tail of his jacket.

Captain Pedro laughed loudly. "They are playing a new game," he said.

"What is the name of the game?" Patsy-O asked.

"It is called "Patsy-O and Rusty Red," the Captain said.

The boys turned and saw the real Patsy-O and the real Rusty Red. They stopped playing and followed them down to the pier.

Here a great surprise awaited them!

The Mayor and councillors were there to see them off. They were dressed in their robes of office. A crowd had gathered. A band began to play. The Mayor made a speech. Then he placed a beautiful collar around the neck of Rusty Red.

Fastened to the collar was a brass plate with the words "Olé! Rusty Red!" upon it.

Just then a shining motor-car drew up beside them.

Out stepped the famous matador who had been injured in the arena. His brother Maxim helped him along. The bullfighter's face was pale and his right arm was in a sling. In his left hand he carried a cardboard box wrapped in red and yellow paper.

"This box you are to open when when you come in sight of your own green land," the bullfighter told Patsy-O. "It is my gift to you for having saved my life!"

"It was Rusty Red who saved your life," Patsy-O said.

"That is true," the matador said patting the red setter on the head, "but you are the master who trained him. If you had not followed your dog to Spain, I would have lost my life."

"Go raibh maith agat, a dhuine uasail," Patsy-O said—which means 'Thank you, sir' in Irish. But the matador did not understand Irish, so Patsy-O said "Muchas gracias, Señor Matador." Everybody was pleased then.

Captain Pedro, his crew, Patsy-O and Rusty Red went on board the trawler. The Captain placed the gift parcel in the wheelhouse. There it would be safe during the voyage.

He took Patsy-O into the wheelhouse too. When the engine was started he told the boy to sound the hooter. This was a sign that the trawler was leaving the pier.

Patsy-O pulled on the cord: "Boo-oo-oo-ooh!" the hooter went.

All other trawlers said goodbye by blowing

their hooters. The harbour was filled with glad noise.

Rusty Red ran up and down the deck barking with joy.

As they sailed away, the band played and the crowds cheered. The councillors raised their funny hats. The Mayor and the matador stood side by side on the pier until the trawler was out of sight.

The trawler sailed north. Soon there were no other ships to be seen on the sea. Captain Pedro then allowed Patsy-O to take the wheel and steer the vessel. The weather was beautiful and the sea was calm. After two days Patsy-O came on deck early one morning. He saw the hills of Ireland on the horizon.

It was the morning of St Patrick's Day.

As the boy and his dog stood there watching the land draw nearer, Captain Pedro said. "Now is the time to open the gift parcel."

"I almost forgot!" said Patsy-O.

When the parcel was opened everyone gasped with joy.

There was a beautiful green "suit of lights" that fitted Patsy-O exactly. A three-cornered hat too! And a cape and a stick! And breeches and stockings! And shining shoes with buckles of silver!

The suit also had a secret pocket in which was a purse filled with money which Patsy-O had got in the arena.

When the boy was dressed in the "suit of lights" he looked very handsome. He stood proudly on the deck as they entered the harbour of home.

Rusty Red was barking loudly. He was rushing here and there waiting for the moment when he would jump ashore.

On the pier Old Salt was asleep on the fish box. When he opened one eye he saw the trawler. Then he said sleepily—

A bullfighter and a bow-wow-wow,
Heaven help Moloney's cow.

Snip-Snip the cricket was in the crack in the wall behind the fireplace in the cottage kitchen. He heard Rusty Red barking. He hopped out of his hiding place. Then he popped right into the ear of Banjo the cat who was asleep on the hearth.

The cricket wished to say, "Snip-snip! Rusty is on the ship."

Banjo woke up. He too listened to the distant barking. Then he rushed out into the pantry and began to pluck the bicycle spokes. "Pink-a-pong," the spokes said. What the cat really meant to say was "Pink-a-pong from across the foam, come along, our master is home."

This sound woke up Break o' Day in the ivy bush. The black and yellow cock began to crow at the top of his voice.

What people heard was "Cock-a-doodle-doo." What the cock was really saying was "Cock-a-doodle-doo. Patsy-O is home with the crew!"

All this noise woke up Liberator the donkey. "Hee-haw haw-hee," the donkey brayed. What he meant to say was "Hee-haw, haw-hee: Master and dog are back from sea."

Using his lips, the donkey drew the bolt on his stable door and galloped out.

The cock leaped onto the donkey's head. The cat jumped onto the donkey's back. The cricket was still in the cat's ear.

All four pets hurried down to the harbour.

The noise woke Patsy-O's mother and sister. Hearing Rusty Red barking, they dressed themselves as quickly as they could. They hurried down to the pier. The neighbours came running too.

Mr O'Hay the schoolmaster was in a great hurry. He put on his bowler hat and his shoes, but forgot to change out of his nightshirt. So he had to race home again and change into his Sunday best. Neighbours too joined in the race.

All the boys and girls were out to join in the welcome home. There was no school that day. It was a holiday in honour of St Patrick.

The trawler drew up alongside the pier. A large crowd was waiting. They were all very excited. Everyone knew Rusty Red at once. But where on earth was Patsy-O?

The boy's mother and his sister Ita, were looking every where on the trawler. They could not see Patsy-O. And who was that proud Spanish-looking boy who stood on deck? He was dressed in a wonderful green "suit of lights."

Even the pets were puzzled.

Old Salt solved the riddle. Opening his two eyes together, something no one had ever seen him do before, he pointed his finger at the wee matador.

Then he said in a shaky kind of voice—

Silk, satin, and calico
That matador is Patsy-O!

Everyone cheered. Patsy-O's mother and his sister, Ita, scrambled on board the trawler. They hugged the wanderer and petted the dog who had been lost and found.

Rusty Red was barking and jumping for joy. The donkey began to dance so that the cat and the cock and the cricket had to hold on for dear life.

Mr O'Hay, the schoolmaster was very excited. He even thought he was in school! He went around asking questions twenty to the the dozen.

He asked questions about wigwams and igloos and skyscrapers and battleships. No one had time to answer these questions. But Mr O'Hay kept on asking them just the same.

Captain Pedro raised his hand for silence. First he made a bow. Then he began to speak.

"Amigos!" he said. "Patsy-O and Rusty Red have been very brave in the sunny land of Spain. They saved the life of a famous bullfighter. The Mayor and people of my town send you greetings. Let us give three cheers for the heroes."

"Hip hip horray!"

"Hip hip horray!"

"Hip hip horray!"

The pets could not cheer like real people. But they did the best they could in their own way. Other trawlermen joined in the applause. All in all, it was a very happy beginning to St Patrick's Day.

Everyone hurried home to be ready for church and the procession in the afternoon.

Captain Pedro and the crew said they would take their siesta first and join the others later. They went below the deck to their bunks to have their midday snooze.

Patsy-O, his mother and Ita, and, of course, the five pets set off for the cottage by the beach. On the way home Patsy-O stopped to pick some shamrock in Mother Moloney's field.

He climbed the gate of the field and began to pick some sprigs. The cross-patch cow turned and glared at him.

Then the cow saw that Patsy-O was wearing a bullfighter's suit! And that Rusty Red was watching through the bars of the gate. So she turned away and pretended to be eating grass.

Just then Mother Moloney came out of her small thatched house. In her hand she carried a white gallon filled with creamy milk. "I was too old to go to the pier and welcome you home," she told the boy. "So here is a Patrick's Pot from my Kerry cow and myself!"

"You will all be friends from this day forward," she added. "My cow and I will let you pick all the mushrooms and cowslips and blackberries you want."

"Moo!" said the cow, which meant "Yes, indeed."

Patsy-O took the white gallon of creamy milk. He said "Muchas gracias!" thinking he was in Spain. Then he said *"Go raibh maith agat!"* thinking he was in school. At last he said, "Thanks very much!" to Mother Moloney in English.

"What is a Patrick's Pot?" Patsy-O asked the old lady.

"Well!" Mother Moloney said, "An Easter Egg, a Christmas Box and a Patrick's Pot— that's how the people long ago named the gifts they gave to children on feast days."

"Thank you, and your cow for a lovely Patrick's Pot,"said Patsy-O. Turning to Rusty Red he said "Wag your tail, Rusty Red."

The red setter wagged his tail. This was to show that he too wished to be friends with Mrs Moloney and her cow.

Patsy-O began to pick more shamrock. He soon had enough and to spare for everyone. Then they went off home to make ready for the procession.

What a happy procession that was! Patsy-O walked in front. He was wearing the "suit of lights." He also wore his shamrock and harp.

His mother, his sister and Captain Pedro marched close beside him.

The pets came next. Master O'Hay led the schoolchildren.

Then came the crews of the trawlers followed by the neighbours.

Lastly came the piper's band. The pipers were dressed in green and red and gold and blue. The band was playing a marching air.

The procession halted near a platform on the village square right in front of the church. Patsy-O and Ita went up the steps to the stage and danced a reel.

Captain Pedro and his crew then danced a Spanish dance. It was called a flamenco. The men had no castanets but they clicked their fingers instead.

Mother Moloney brought along her milking stool. She sat on it and clapped her hands in time with the music.

The children sang "Hail Glorious St Patrick." Mr O'Hay was the conductor of the school choir.

When the concert was over everyone marched down to the pier. They wished to say goodbye to Captain Pedro and the crew of his trawler. The vessel sailed away into the setting sun.

Then the people went home, tired but full of joy after a wonderful day.

* * * *

Night had fallen when again the family returned to the little cottage by the beach. The waves said "Whoosh!" as they fell and broke.

After supper Snip-Snip hopped out of the cat's ear. He slipped into the crack in the wall. The rest of the pets went to their sleeping places.

Patsy-O sat on his stool. He told his mother and his sister, Ita, of his adventures. He told them about the fiesta and the siesta. He gave his mother the purse of money from the Secret Pocket of the "suit of lights."

Rusty Red was fast asleep on the flag of the hearth. He began to bark in his sleep. He was dreaming that he was hanging onto the bull's tail in the arena in Spain. And that the crowds were cheering as he and his master paraded around.

After a time Ita went off to bed. Then Patsy-O's head dropped on his breast. Before long he was fast asleep.

His mother lifted him gently and laid him on the bed. She took off his "suit of lights" and hung it carefully in the wardrobe.

Then she tucked the bedclothes around her son and closed the bedroom door without making a sound.

When she had closed the cottage door she could no longer hear the sound of the sea. It was very quiet in the kitchen then. The children breathing gently in their sleep. Hmmmmm! Mnnmnh! they went just like that.

The widow began to smile with joy.

Once again the little cottage was filled with peace.

Everyone was safely home and Patsy-O's mother and sister, and Patsy-O himself together with his five wonderful pets were again as happy and as happy and as happy and as happy and as happy as the lovely days are

L O N G.

High in the Sky with Patsy-O

High in the Sky with Patsy-O

"The wild geese are making ready to leave the lake," his mother said to Patsy-O. The widow was looking out the window of the cottage. The little house stood beside the sea and the lake.

"I shall be lonely when the wild geese have gone," Patsy-O said.

"I shall be lonely too," said Ita his sister.

"I like to go down to the lake every day after school and watch them," the boy said.

"It's April now. It's time for the geese to fly away," his mother said.

"Where do they go?" Patsy-O wanted to know.

"To Greenland in the far north-west," the widow said.

"Why do they go to Greenland?" Ita asked.

"The ice will soon be melting on the lakes of

Greenland. The snow will be thawing on the hills. Plants will be growing to provide food for the wild geese. There on a level place without trees called a tundra they will build their nests and rear their goslings."

"Will the wild geese return?" both children asked.

"In October when the weather in Greenland gets very cold and the lakes are frozen over, the geese will return to our own lake to spend the winter here with us again."

"Eskimos live in Greenland," Patsy-O's sister, Ita, said. "I've read about them in my book at school."

"I would like to visit the Eskimos," Patsy-O said.

The children and their mother sat by the turf fire. They had eaten their supper. Darkness was falling over the little cove where the waves of the sea rose up and crashed down on the sand with a mighty "Whoosh." When their mother lighted the lamp the kitchen was safe and warm.

Patsy-O's pets too were safe and warm.

Snip-Snip the cricket was cosy in a crack in the wall behind the fireplace.

Banjo the cat had stopped plucking the spokes of a bicycle as if it were a banjo. He had curled up for a nap beside the hearth.

Break o' Day, the black and gold cock who crowed at daybreak was safe in his ivy bush.

Rusty Red the Irish setter was snoozing in his kennel. The kennel was near the workshop in which Patsy-O's father, a carpenter, had once made tables and chairs.

The father, alas, was now dead, but Patsy-O had learned some carpentry from his Daddy when he was alive.

Liberator the Donkey was still nibbling grass in a field beside the house. The mother looked up at the clock.

"It's time to put Liberator in his stable," she said. "There may be a thick fog tonight."

"He will liberate himself in the morning," Patsy-O said. "He will draw back the bolt with his whiskery lips. I shall lead him in just the same."

The boy put on his Aran sweater and his cap with the pom-poms.

A thick fog had settled over the sand and the sea. Patsy-O could only see a short distance before his face. High above the fog he could hear the beating of many wings.

"The geese have left the lake," Patsy-O told himself. He heard their cries: "Kow-lie-ow" and "Lie-o-lie-ok."

"The wild geese are lost in the fog," Patsy-O's mother said.

"Do not get lost yourself, Patsy-O," his sister added. They closed the cottage door to keep out the dense fog.

Patsy-O stood quite still. He heard the sound of the sea, the beating of wings and the cackling of the birds. Above him in the sky the geese were circling, but he could not see them.

A ghostly shape loomed up out of the mist. Patsy-O saw that it was Liberator, his donkey. The boy caught the animal by the forelock and led him towards the open door of the stable.

Suddenly the beating of wings was just above the boy's head. The cry of birds filled the air about him. He heard the thump of wings.

Some of the geese had flown blindly into the donkey's stable.

"What is it?" Patsy-O's mother called out. She was standing in the cottage doorway. Ita was close beside her.

"Sssh, mother," Patsy-O said. "Some of the wild geese have flown into the stable. They cannot find their way through the fog." When the boy tiptoed in he could hear the wild geese moving about in the darkness. A gust of wind from the sea blew against the stable door so that it closed.

The geese flew wildly from wall to wall over the boy's head.

Patsy-O made a noose of the reins and spread it on the stable floor.

Still holding the rope he crept into corner of the stable. He could hear the geese coming together. "Lie-lie-ok" they said. They rested their long necks on each other.

A gust of wind blew open the stable door. The white fog streamed in. The geese flapped their wings. As they did so Patsy-O drew the noose tight around the legs of the geese.

The great birds struggled to be free. Patsy-O held on to the reins for dear life. He wound the loose end of the rope around his wrist and arm.

The birds pulled Patsy-O after them through the doorway and out into the mist. There were five geese in all. They flew up in the sky, pulling Patsy-O behind them.

Glancing down, Patsy-O could barely see his mother and sister in the doorway of the little cottage. "I shall be back to play the games on Hallowe'en," he shouted as they waved him goodbye.

Up flew the birds. Up and up through the fog. Patsy-O could hear a flock of geese cackling and calling far above. The five birds rose above the mist. They came out where the stars were winking and the moon shone brightly in the night sky.

They joined a huge flock of wild geese. The geese were circling in the heavens. They honked and cackled and welcomed the five birds who had been lost. The strong wings of the geese beat above and below Patsy-O. The air from their wings held him up. The strain of the rope on his wrist and arm did not now seem so great.

Patsy-O found that he was flying. He did not feel cold: the feathers of the wild geese kept his body warm.

An old gander honked loudly and began to fly to the north west. He was the leader. The rest of the flock followed.

The geese were strong: they flew as if Patsy-O was a light load.

Now and again a young gander flew down and looked at Patsy-O with his beady eye. The bird *seemed* to be saying "Now you can fly just like us." But all the young gander said was "Lie-lie-ok" and "Honk honk." He then flew off to join the others.

Patsy-O felt drowsy. A huge bank of cloud lay below. He felt quite safe. Soon he fell fast asleep.

When he awoke he saw the sun rising in the

east. It was like a ball of fire. The flock of birds was touched with the red of dawn. Patsy-O looked down.

He could see fields and houses far below. A motor car looked like a toy. He saw a lighthouse on the coast. By now it was broad day. Soon the geese and the boy were over the ocean.

An aeroplane flew towards them. The flock of geese just flew on and on. Patsy-O could see the pilot in the cockpit. The man had his nose pressed closed to the glass. The passengers were looking out the windows of the plane.

They could not believe their eyes. A real boy flying with wild geese! Were they dreaming?

Then the aeroplane was gone.

Hour after hour passed. The geese flew on and on. Patsy-O felt quite comfortable.

Time passed. The air grew colder. Patsy-O shivered—but only just a little. When he looked down he saw broken ice floating on the sea. He saw a huge iceberg.

Then they came to a land covered with snow and ice. "This must be Greenland," Patsy-O told himself. "I think it should have been named Whiteland," he said then. The birds flew westward over the frozen land.

Soon all the geese started to cackle and

honk. The old gander who was leading the flock began to go down. The flock moved in a wide circle above a long arm of the sea which is called a fjord. There were patches of ice on the water below. "I hope my geese know where to land," Patsy-O said to himself as he saw some of the birds landing with a splash on a lake beside the fjord.

As if the geese on his reins had heard him they landed on the lakeside. Patsy-O hit the ground with a little thump. The snow was like a cushion so he was not hurt. He freed the geese. The boy looked around him. Such cackling and honking and humming was never heard before.

My, but it was cold. "What shall I do now?" Patsy-O asked himself.

He saw a small boat crossing from the other side of the fjord. In it was a small man dressed in furs. He was rowing with a paddle and moving in and out through the ice floes.

"That boat is a kayak," Patsy-O said to himself. "The man is an Eskimo."

When the kayak came close to where Patsy-O stood the man stopped rowing.

The man was old. He had a yellowish face and black hair cut to a fringe under a fur hood. He looked at Patsy-O. He looked at the geese.

He looked up at the sky. He scratched his nose and stepped ashore.

"Where you come from, boy?" the old fellow asked.

"I come from Ireland?" Patsy-O replied.

"How you come from Ireland?"

"I flew here with the wild geese."

The old fellow pushed back his hood. He scratched his head. "My kayak is small," he said. "I get for you a bigger boat."

The man raised his paddle and swung it back and forth three times.

A bigger boat left the far shore. "Phut-phut" went the engine of the large boat. It had a younger man on board.

He took Patsy-O and the old man on board the larger boat. They tied the kayak to a rope and towed it behind them. They went back across the fjord.

"We are Eskimos," the old man said. "My name is Itok which means grandfather."

"You are welcome to Greenland," the other said. "My name is Shappa. I am his son. I have two children, a boy called Mittek and a girl called Meeka."

When they reached the village on the other side all the people came out. They crowded round the boy from Ireland. Everyone, even the children, was dressed in furs.

"How you come?" they asked again.

"I flew with the wild geese," Patsy-O said.

The children laughed. "You have no wings," they said.

Patsy-O told how he had caught five geese in a noose of his donkey's reins. And how they had taken him with them on their flight to Greenland.

"We have never seen a donkey," the little boy called Mittek said.

"Have you seen a Polar Bear?" his sister asked the Irish lad. Her name was Meeka.

"I have seen one in the Zoo," Patsy-O said.

"What is your name?" the two children asked.

"My name is Patsy-O from Ireland."

Grandfather Itok said, "Hush! The boy is tired and hungry. He can talk later."

Some of the houses were neat timber huts. But others were round in shape and were made of blocks of snow. Patsy-O knew that these were called igloos.

"You like to go in a house or an igloo?" old Itok asked.

"If you please, I would like to go into an igloo," Patsy-O said.

The children were pleased at this. Mittek

and his sister, Meeka, took Patsy-O by the
hand and led him to their igloo.

They stopped beside a low door.

The children went on their hands and knees.
Patsy-O followed. It was like crawling through
a tunnel. They passed a small storehouse
where seal meat was kept. Patsy-O stood up
inside the igloo.

Nannoo, the Eskimo mother, welcomed him.
Shappa, the Eskimo Daddy, brought some
fish. The boy had a lovely meal of hot fish soup.
Afterwards he felt tired.

"Now for a sleep," the Eskimo mother said.

"Where shall I sleep?" Patsy-O asked.

"On this frozen bench of snow."

"Will I be cold?" the boy asked.

"Oh, no. When the bench is covered with seal
skins and furs you will be very comfortable."

"Why is the day so long?" Patsy-O asked.

"The days are getting longer just now,"
Shappa, the Eskimo Daddy said. "Before long
the sun will never set so there will be very little
darkness. In winter the nights are very long
and there is very little daylight."

Patsy-O yawned. He felt sleepy. The fire was
in the middle of the floor. The smoke curled out
through a hole in the roof of the igloo. There
was a lamp of seal oil.

The mother threw lots of furs on the bench of snow.

"Off to bed, Patsy-O," she said.

Nannoo covered the boy with seal skins. He could hardly keep his eyes open. Other children crept through the tunnel and peeped at the Irish boy.

He felt as snug as a bug in a rug.

Soon he was fast asleep.

He dreamt of home. Of his mother and his sister, Ita. He had promised to be home for Hallowe'en which was a long way off. Could he keep his promise?

He also dreamt of his five pets.

Snip-Snip the cricket would find an igloo cold.

Banjo the cat would sleep among the furs. But there were no mice in an igloo.

There was no bush in which Break o' Day, his cock, could shelter.

Liberator the donkey wore small iron shoes. He would slip and fall on the ice.

As for Rusty Red, his setter, what dogs the boy had seen were great hairy huskies who drew sleighs across the snow. They would give his dog a bad time.

When Patsy-O awoke he wasn't quite sure where he was. Then he realized that he was in Greenland.

He heard a shout from outside. "A fish, a fish," the voice said.

The children scrambled out. Above a hole in the ice a red flag was waving. One of the boys skated out on the thick ice. Tied to the flag was a fishing line. Caught on a hook on the fishing line was a fine fish.

What a wonderful breakfast they had then. Water was dripping from the roof onto the fire.

"The weather is growing warm. Soon we shall go into our houses," Nannoo, the mother Eskimo said.

As they were finishing the meal they heard a mighty noise. Patsy-O thought it was thunder. All the children ran out and watched as a great frozen cliff of snow collapsed into the fjord. A huge spout of water rose into the air. Then they saw a great block of ice floating on the sea.

The wild geese took fright at the sound. They rose into the air. They circled in the sky and then returned to their places.

"That's how icebergs are made," Itok, the old Eskimo said. "Only a small part of the iceberg is seen above the water. They float out to sea. Deep down the ice has sharp edges. Some of the greatest ships on the sea have been torn apart by icebergs."

"I have never seen an iceberg in Ireland." Patsy-O said.

"The icebergs float southward. Then they melt in the warmer water," old Itok said.

After a few days Patsy-O was used to the new way of life. He wore sealskin clothes like the other young Eskimos. He was given short green wellies. He still wore the knitted cap with the pom-poms.

He played with the children of the village.

One day they got very excited.

"See! See!" they shouted pointing out to the breaking ice.

At first Patsy-O could see nothing. Then he spied a large white animal floating along on a block of ice.

It was a Polar bear.

The children raced towards the bank of the river. They kept their heads low so that the bear could not see them. Patsy-O followed.

"Sssh!" the children said as they crouched behind a bank of snow. "The bear will soon be hunting."

The bear got off the raft of ice. He walked

along the shore where the ice had melted.

Suddenly the bear stood quite still. The children saw him leap into the water. His head went down. When the head came up a seal was seen wriggling in the bear's mouth. The bear walked to the river bank and began to eat the seal.

But he only ate a small part of it. The rest he left on the shore and then ambled off to catch more seals. One of the children crept forward. He took out a knife and sliced off the marks of the bear's teeth on the seal.

All began to hurry home with their prize.

On the way home Patsy-O was silent. Meeka, the Eskimo girl asked, "What is troubling you, Patsy-O?"

"I was just wondering," Patsy-O said.

"What were you wondering about?" Mittek asked.

"I go to school in my own country. Mr O'Hay is my teacher. You never seem to go to school. All you do is listen to the radio."

"We attend school," the Eskimo children said with a smile.

"Where is your school?"

"Our school is high in the sky," the boy said.

The Irish lad looked up. He saw no school in the sky. Then Mittek said. "Ours is a radio

school. We learn our lessons from a teacher
who lives far away. He will be here today. The
doctor will be here too. Hurry or we shall be
late."

As the children hurried back to the village
they heard the noise of an aeroplane in the sky.
"Burrum-burrum"—just like that.

The geese flew off in different directions.
The aeroplane circled and came down low over
the part of the fjord where the ice had melted.

"It will crash in the water," Patsy-O said.

"This plane has floats instead of wheels,"
Mittek explained. "It is a sea plane. If there
was ice on the lake it would have skis to help it
land safely."

"I understand," Patsy-O said.

The plane skimmed low and then landed on
the water. It did not sink, of course, as the
floats kept it up. It taxied through the ice floes
to the landing-place.

All the people of the village came out to
welcome the visitors.

First came a man with a leather bag.

"Welcome, doctor," the people said.

Next came a lady with a white veil. She also
had a leather case.

"Welcome, nurse," all the people said.

Next came a man with a large satchel of

books.

"Welcome, teacher," all the people said.

All marched up to the village hall. The doctor looked at Patsy-O.

"Oho," he said. "Who have we here?"

"My name is Patsy-O," the boy replied.

"Where are you from, my boy?"

"From Ireland, doctor."

The doctor put on his spectacles. "How did you come here?" he asked, looking keenly at Patsy-O.

"I came with the white-fronted geese, doctor."

"You mean you can fly?"

Patsy-O told the story of how the great birds took him with them across the ocean to Greenland.

"Bless my soul," the doctor said. "I never heard the like of that." The teacher and the nurse were very surprised too.

"Do you wish to fly back with us to the city?" the doctor asked. "There we can put you on a jumbo jet that is flying to Ireland."

"Oh, no!" all the Eskimo children said. "No-no-no-no-no. Please let him stay here."

"How will he get home then?" the teacher asked.

"Patsy-O will return with the wild geese just

as he came" the children answered.

"Yes," Patsy-O said. "Our winter is not as cold as yours. The geese spend it on a lake beside my home. I shall go home just as I came."

"Well, well, well," doctor and teacher and nurse said together. "We never heard the like of that."

"I shall be at home in time to play the games at Hallowe'en. My sister, Ita, shall wear a tall hat and a mask and we shall have lots of fun," Patsy-O said.

The nurse said, "The teacher has a radio station to talk to his big class all over Greenland. He can speak to your country and send word to your folks that you are safe and well."

"What a splendid idea," the doctor said.

"Leave it to me," the teacher said. "Come along, children. I must see what progress you have been making for the past month."

Patsy-O joined the class. The doctor and nurse were preparing to examine the children.

"I shall begin with an easy problem," the teacher said. He drew a small lake on the blackboard. He drew a pole standing in the middle of the water. He drew a coil of rope on the the bank.

"Listen carefully," the teacher said. "I wish to put a noose around the pole. Here is the rope. I cannot swim. I cannot throw the rope like a lasso. I cannot use a boat nor an aeroplane. How do I do it?"

The Eskimo children guessed and guessed. None of them was right.

Patsy-O remembered how he had caught the wild geese with the donkey's reins.

"Do you know how to do it, Patsy-O?" the teacher asked.

"Yes, sir."

"Stand in front of the class. Explain how the problem is solved."

Patsy-O said: "I would make a loop at one end of the rope. Taking the other end of the rope I would walk all round the lake to where I started. I would pull the loose end through the loop. Then I would have a lasso."

"What then?" the teacher asked.

"I would pull on the loose end. The noose would move through the water and tighten around the pole."

"Good boy!" the teacher said. All the children clapped their hands.

"Perhaps you have a riddle for us," the teacher said.

"Yes, sir," Patsy-O said. "This riddle is a

word in the form of a rhyme." Then he began:

Three-fourths of a cross and a circle
complete

Two semi-circles a perpendicular
meet.

Next comes a triangle which stands
on two feet,

Two more semi-circles and a circle
complete.

The children tried very hard but they could not find the word. Even the teacher was puzzled. "We give up," the boys and girls shouted.

Patsy-O took the chalk and explained the word on the the blackboard.

Three-fourths of a cross—that's the letter T

A circle complete—that's the letter O

Two semi-circles a perpendicular
meet—that's B

A triangle that stands on two feet
(The children shouted)—that's A

Two more semi-circles—those are C

and C

And a circle complete (The children
shouted) O

So Patsy-O wrote the mystery word on the blackboard—

TOBACCO

After this Patsy-O was something of a hero. He took care not to appear proud.

There was a knock on the schoolroom door. The nurse came in. "The doctor will examine each one of you in turn," she told the children.

Some of the boys and girls had coughs. Others had colds in their noses. Some had slight pains in the tummies. These were given small doses of medicine. One boy had a broken hand: he had fallen on the ice. The doctor had skilful hands. He set the broken bone in its place and then bound it up in plaster so that the bone would knit again.

"You are a fine healthy lad," the doctor told Patsy-O when he had finished his examination.

The grown-up people were also examined.

As the mothers waited with their babies for injections Patsy-O saw one mother and baby play a little game.

The mother had made a small circle of whalebone. She gave the baby a straight bone. The baby tried to poke the straight bone into the circle. It was a simple game: for the baby it was quite difficult.

When the baby poked the bone into the circle all the other babies crowed and chuckled with delight.

The teacher gave the children homework for the following month.Then all the people went down to the pier. The flock of geese took no notice. Doctor, teacher and nurse boarded the seaplane. "Please don't forget to radio my home," Patsy-O said.

"We won't forget," they said.

"Tell them that I hope my five pets are well," he added.

The propellers of the plane began to turn. The plane moved along the open water on its floats. Then it rose into the air. The Eskimos waved until the plane was out of sight.

As the villagers were returning home they heard a great noise coming from the sea. A spout of water was shooting up from the waves. The noise was like the snoring of a giant. Patsy-O and the children ran to the beach.

"There she goes: there she blows," the Eskimo children shouted.

"What is it?" Patsy-O asked.

"It's a whale," the boys and girls said. They could see the great dark curve of the whale's back. They saw the spout of water and they heard the snore. The great tail waved in the water. After a time the whale swam out to sea.

That was not the only noise the boy heard.

When Patsy-O woke it was quite bright though it was really early in the morning. He heard a loud noise that sounded like BONK. There was a pause. Then came the noise of rushing in the snow outside and again the BONK.

Patsy-O rose and crept to the window of ice. He cleaned the window as best he could. Then he peeped out.

He saw a herd of deer. He knew they were called caribou. Two of the bulls had great antlers.

The bulls went back some distance from each other. Then they rushed forward to attack. "BONK," the bulls banged their heads together.

"What are they doing?" Patsy-O asked Mittek who had come up beside him.

"The bulls are fighting to see who will be king of the herd," the boy said.

"BONK," went the noise again as the heads banged together.

After a while one of the bulls turned tail and walked away. Perhaps he would be king of another herd of caribou when he got bigger and stronger.

With all these adventures Patsy-O did not miss the time passing. Every day there was some excitement. A ride in a kayak or fishing for salmon. Patsy-O asked his Eskimo friends many questions But, of course, the young Eskimos asked him questions also.

"Have you igloos in Ireland?"

"Are there polar bears in your country?"

"Do you hunt seals like we do?"

"Do you wear skins instead of clothes?"

"Tell us all about your pets."

"Is Rusty Red a huskie?"

"Have you a school in the sky?"

Patsy-O told about his life in Ireland. He told about his mother and his sister, Ita.

He said he lived in a small cottage with a roof of straw which was called thatch. Sparrows made their nest in the thatch.

There were no igloos in Ireland. Not much frost and snow either.

There were no polar bears.

A seal sometimes put up its head in the cove near his home.

Patsy-O then played on a tin whistle. The seal seemed to listen to the music.

Then it dived under the waves.

The boy said he did not wear skins. But his mother knitted sweaters and caps out of sheep's wool.

He told about his pets.

Rusty Red was not a huskie. If there was

snow Patsy-O sat on a tray on the hillside.
Catching the setter's tail he would shout "Hie
for home, Rusty Red." The clever dog would
pull him home.

Patsy-O told the children about Mother
Moloney's cross-patch cow who chased Rusty
Red out of her field. But when Rusty caught
her by the tail she ended the chase.

He told about his donkey bringing turf or
peat from the bog to burn in the winter fires.

He told them about Master O'Hay, the
schoolmaster, who had lots of riddles.

He told the children that he liked porridge
and cream for breakfast.

He told them that his mother baked soda
bread in a round pot oven beside the glowing
fire.

The Eskimo children listened very carefully.

Then Mittek said, "Tomorrow is the 'Day of
the Young Ones'."

"What Young Ones?" Patsy-O said.

"Wait till morning, Patsy-O," the children
said with laughter.

Patsy-O was up at the crack of dawn.

With his two special friends, Mittek and
Meeka, Patsy-O walked to the head of the
fjord. They came to the place where the geese
were nesting beside the lake.

The geese set up a great hullabaloo when they saw them approaching. They cackled and honked. The ganders hissed loudly.

The mother geese were sitting on their nests on the tundra beside the water. They were hatching their eggs. The father geese were out searching for food. An old gander was on guard.

Patsy-O spied his own special five geese. Two of the geese sat on their nests. Others were eating grass and sedge. Old Grandfather Gander strutted about. He looked fierce.

A large boat appeared on the water. With cries of alarm the flock of geese rose into the air.

"Now is our chance," Mittek said.

The children hurried towards a nest. There were four lovely eggs in the nest. "I hear something," the boy said to them. The children heard a tapping noise.

"A gosling is trying to break out of the shell," Meeka said. "I shall help it."

Very carefully she took up the egg. Just then the shell broke at a small point and a little yellow beak appeared. The girl picked off bits of the shell beside the beak. Her fingers worked gently.

The children saw a small eye. Then they saw a small head. Then they saw a lovely grey-green gosling step out of the broken shell.

The girl laid the little fledgling on the nest beside the eggs.

"How lovely it is!" she said.

But the geese were coming back. "We must hurry off," Mittek said. "We are your friends," Patsy-O called out as the flock of birds returned.

The children then ran up a hill of snow. They lay down behind a drift. They peeped down into the valley on the other side.

"Ssh," they said.

Patsy-O peeped over the edge. He could see nothing except snow.

One of the children whispered, "Look." He pointed across the valley.

At the bottom of the hill just opposite to where the children were lying the snow was beginning to move. It heaved and crumbled and humped. Then a small hill of snow came up out of the ground. When the snow fell down they saw it was a mother Polar bear.

She had come up out of her den under the snow.

The bear turned her head this way and that. She sniffed the air.

The bear had black eyes, a black nose and small ears.

She had sharp claws. Her body was covered with white fur. At her shoulders she was as high as a man's chest.

Again she smelled the wind. The children bent down.

"Sssh," Mittek said again.

The bear lumbered back to the hole and made a sound.

A cub appeared. It looked like a white football of fur. A second cub came up. A third put up its head.

Soon the three cubs and their mother were playing in the snow.

Such tumbling and tossing and grumbling and growling and running and rolling. All in fun, of course.

The children could not help laughing. The mother bear made a warning sound. The cubs scuttled down into their den. The mother bear went last. The snow on the sides of the hole fell gently in. The children could only barely see where mother and cubs had been.

It was still the Day of the Young Ones.

The children came to a tall black cliff beside the tundra. They hid behind rocks.

"Look up!" the Eskimo children said.

Patsy-O looked up. He could see a great number of large birds standing by their nests high on the ledges on the face of the cliff. "These are barnacle geese," the Eskimo boy said. "They live on cliffs."

Patsy-O saw that there were many goslings beside their parents. They were too small to fly. How were they to get down? The cliff was as high as the tall steeple of a church.

"Here comes the enemy," Meeka said.

A black and white Arctic fox was skulking among the rocks. "He is waiting for the little ones to come down," Mittek told Patsy-O. "If he catches them he will eat them up."

"Oh!" Patsy-O said. He took up a stick to hunt away the fox.

"Wait," the other children said. "Watch out for falcons too."

Falcons are fierce birds who eat smaller birds. There were some of those about.

High on the cliff a mother goose and a father goose were telling a little bird to jump.

The little bird was afraid. His wings were small. All of a sudden he leaped.

He fell like a ball. He opened his little wings. But he could not fly. He hopped off a rock. When he hit the mossy tundra he bounced like a rubber ball.

The fox ran forward. He opened his cruel jaws. Patsy-O ran with his stick. He shouted at the top of his voice. The fox turned tail and ran off. A falcon came diving down. The father goose and the mother goose chased the falcon over the snow. The little gosling was safe.

Lots of goslings began falling from the cliff. Their mothers picked them up. All waddled off to the lake. A flock of mothers and goslings were soon floating on the water. "They are safe now," the three children said.

They saved many goslings in this way.

There were also baby seals and small walruses with tusks. And hairy musk-ox calves and young caribou deer. So it was really a Day of the Young Ones.

As the children were walking home a strange thing happened.

Patsy-O was wearing his knitted cap. Down from the sky swooped a falcon.

The bird snatched the cap from Patsy-O's head and flew high into the air. The cruel bird thought that the pom-poms were little goslings.

But when he tried to gobble them up he found that the pom-poms were made of wool.

He dropped the cap. It floated down like a parachute. Patsy-O put it on his head and drew it tight down about his ears.

So the days passed in Greenland. The Irish lad was having a splendid time. Before the snow melted he asked how an igloo was made.

Itok, the wise old Eskimo, got a saw. He cut blocks of frozen snow. With these he built a small igloo. Patsy-O helped too. In front of it the older Eskimo placed a notice: PATSY-O'S IGLOO. The children used it as a playhouse.

Shappa built a small sleigh for the Irish boy and harnessed a huskie to it.

"Mush-mush," Patsy-O said. Drawing the sleigh the huskie raced down the hill. The Eskimo father also built a small kayak in which Patsy-O paddled in shallow water.

"I shall have many stories to tell when I go home," Patsy-O said to himself.

"I have seen many animals. I have seen whales and seals, musk-oxen and walruses, Arctic foxes, Polar bears and caribou. I've seen many huskies, of course. I've heard wolves crying in the night. I've seen fox cubs and seal puppies.

I've seen many birds. White-fronted geese and barnacle geese, gulls and kittiwakes. Long-tailed wild ducks and snow owls. And the falcon who tried to steal my pom-poms.

I've eaten all kinds of fish, salmon and cod especially. I've seen seals hunting the fish under the ice. And coming up through holes in the ice to breathe."

By this time plants were growing. The weather was not quite as cold as it had been. There was no night. The sun went round and round in the sky.

The igloos had melted. The Eskimos lived in their houses.

"Does it ever get dark?" Patsy-O asked.

There is no daylight in winter," the children said. "Sometimes we can see the northern lights."

"Are these like a great fan of lights spreading up into the sky?" Patsy-O asked.

"Yes indeed," Mittek and Meeka said together.

Just then Patsy-O remembered. "I've seen them once in my country. They shone over the sea to the north. We called them the 'Roley-boley-Alice' lights."

The other children laughed.

"You are almost right, Patsy-O," Meeka said. "Our teacher says the correct name is 'Aur-o-ra Bor-e-alis' which is the Latin name for these lights."

"I prefer 'Roley-boley-Alice'," Patsy-O said.

"We do too," the two children said. "It's much easier to say."

So all three said "Roley-boley-Alice" together.

Autumn was drawing to an end. The first snowflakes of winter began to fall.

Patsy-O remembered his plan to be home in time to play the games on Hallowe'en.

He told the children of the village that he was about to leave them. When they heard this they were sad—Mittek and Meeka especially.

The Eskimo boy said, "The goslings are big and fat and strong. Instead of five geese to fly you home you will have many companions."

The following day, the people of the village gave Patsy-O some gifts.

Mother Nannoo gave him mittens to keep his fingers warm. Shappa, the father, gave him a toy kayak and a toy sleigh. Old Itok gave him a set of small animals and birds which he had carved from the tusk of a walrus.

These gifts the boy carried in a small sealskin belt tied around his waist.

Everybody, young and old, went with Patsy-O to the lakeside. The boy took with him his donkey's reins.

The geese were making ready to leave. They were cackling and honking and humming. One old gander went around making a great fuss.

The goslings were excited too. It was their first time flying to the lake in Ireland.

Patsy-O said goodbye to his friends. He said a special goodbye to Mittek and Meeka. Then he spread the noose of the reins where his five friendly geese had their nests.

"Lie-o-lie-ok," the geese said.

Patsy-O placed some food in the middle of the loop. He waited behind a small drift of snow.

The five geese came to eat the food. The goslings watched their parents. When all five geese were in the circle—the children shouted "Pull!"

Patsy-O drew the noose tight about the legs of the geese.

The geese were strong. They drew Patsy-O after them. At the edge of the sea all five rose into the air. They pulled Patsy-O up up up into the sky. Again he tied the rope around his wrist and arm.

The goslings came too. Next came the great flock of geese. The beating of their wings kept the boy safely aloft.

Patsy-O looked down. He could see his

friends the Eskimos waving goodbye. With his free hand he also waved goodbye.

The old gander honked an order. The flock turned southeast in the direction of Ireland. The goslings flew quite close to Patsy-O's face.

They flew miles and miles over frozen land. Over islands and icebergs. Over hills and hollows. Soon they were over the great ocean.

Once again Patsy-O fell fast asleep. He felt warm and safe. At last he looked down and saw the coast of Ireland.

There below him was the lake, the beach and his very own cottage.

The officer gander honked. The white-fronted geese spread their great wings and wheeled in the sky. Lower and lower they came.

Patsy-O tugged on the reins so that his geese would not land on the water. Just as he did when he went for a ride on Liberator his donkey.

The geese landed safe and sound on a field beside the lake. Patsy-O untied the rope and let the geese go free. "Thank you, my friends!" he said. "You have taken me safely to Greenland. Now you have brought me safely home."

Just then he heard a loud "Moo" behind him.

It was Mother Moloney's cow. "Moooo," she said again very loudly indeed.

Snip-Snip, the cricket, heard the sound. The clever insect knew it meant something special. He jumped into the ear of Banjo, the cat.

The cat twanged on the bicycle spokes. Break o' Day was just falling asleep in his ivy bush. He woke up and crowed "Cock-a-doodle doo."

Liberator, the donkey, drew the bolt on his stable door with his whiskery lips. He gave a loud hee-haw. Rusty Red bounded out of his kennel and barked as loudly as he could.

Just then the pets heard a whistle. They knew that Patsy-O was home.

Hearing all the hullabaloo Patsy-O's mother and his sister, Ita, came out of the cottage.

The pets had run off. Liberator, the donkey, was first. Break o' Day, the cock, was perched between the donkey's ears. Banjo, the cat, clung to the donkey's back. Snip-Snip, the cricket, was in the cat's ear. Rusty Red, the setter raced along beside them, barking with joy.

"In heaven's name, what's the matter?" the widow asked.

"I'm ho-o-oome, mother," Patsy-O shouted.

"It's Patsy-O, home from Greenland," Ita

said. She and her mother hurried to the
lakeside. "Welcome home!" they said as they
kissed and hugged the boy. "The radio told us
that you were well," his mother said.

The pets showed their love in their own way.
The crosspatch cow ran off when she saw
Rusty Red.

"Just in time for Hallowe'en," Ita said.

"After supper we shall have the games," the
mother said.

"And I shall show you all my gifts," said
Patsy-O.

Patsy-O turned to his friends, the wild
geese. "I shall come to see you every day," he
said. Patsy-O then brought along the reins.
They all trooped back to the cottage.

The boy had a big bowl of hot broth and some
home baked bread.

He felt much better then. The pets had a
meal too. They then went to their sleeping
places.

Patsy-O showed his mother and Ita the
mittens, the toy kayak and the toy sleigh. He
also showed the little animals and birds carved
out of ivory. "They are all beautiful," they said.

"Now for the fun," the mother said. They
began to play Hallowe'en games.

Ita put on a tall black hat. She wore a wide

skirt. She placed a mask on her face. She had the handle of a brush as a broomstick.

"I'm a witch," she said. "I can fly through the air."

"You'll never never fly to Greenland," said Patsy-O.

"I can try," said Ita. She gave a small hop on the floor. She was laughing.

The children's mother tied a piece of twine to a hook in the ceiling. She tied a red rosy apple to the end of the cord.

"See if you can take a bite out of the apple with your hands behind your backs," the mother said.

Patsy-O tried. He failed to bite the apple.

Ita caught the fruit between her chin and shoulder. She took a big bite out of the apple. She won this game.

The mother then placed a silver coin in a shallow pan of water. "Hands behind the backs again," she said. "Who can take up the coin?"

Ita tried to take it up with her mouth. Her hair fell into the water. She stopped trying then.

Patsy-O bent down. He had short hair. He brought up the coin in his lips.

After this the mother cut the barm brack. She gave a slice to each of the children. Ita found a ring in her slice.

"You will be married when you are a young woman," Mammy told her.

Patsy-O sliced the top off a turnip. He scooped out its centre. He cut two eyes, a nose and a mouth in the face of the vegetable.

He placed a small candle into the hollow turnip. He lighted the candle. Then he put back the sliced top.

He placed the turnip on the little bridge beside the cottage. Mother Moloney's cow came along to the fence. She sniffed.

"If she could only get over the fence she would eat the turnip," Ita said.

Two fishermen were passing in a boat. One stopped rowing. "Is that a ghost?" he asked. He was afraid.

The other man laughed. "It's a candle in a turnip," he said. "Patsy-O must have come back from Greenland."

Just then Patsy-O saw the northern lights in the sky. He thought of his Eskimo friends.

"Before you go to bed, tell us of your adventures," the mother told her son.

Patsy-O sat on his three-legged stool. He told his mother and Ita of his adventures.

He told how the geese had flown him to Greenland. He told all about his friends the

Eskimos, especially Mittek and Meeka, the boy and girl. He told about the igloos and the fishing flag, the kayaks and the Polar bears. He told about the Day of the Young Ones and the falcon who tried to eat his pom-poms.

He told about the doctor and the nurse and the school in the sky. And lots more besides.

"You must tell this story to the other children at school," his mother said.

"Mr O'Hay will be pleased that you answered all the questions," Ita said. "And that you had a riddle for the children."

"We are very proud of you," his mother told Patsy-O.

Patsy-O felt very happy then.

By and by he felt sleepy. Ita had already gone to bed.

At last Patsy-O's head dropped on his breast. Before long he was fast asleep.

His mother lifted him gently and laid him on his warm bed. She tucked the bedclothes around him. She closed the bedroom door without making a sound.

She walked to the half-door and looked out at the starry night.

The waves are turning quietly on the little beach. The turnip face was glowing in the dark. The northern lights were fading away.

All the pets were asleep: Liberator in his stable, Rusty Red in the kennel, Break o' Day in the ivy bush, Banjo before the kitchen fire and Snip-Snip in a crack of the wall at the back of the hob.

Patsy-O and Ita too were fast asleep.

The mother closed the door of the cottage. She began to smile with joy. Once again the little cottage was filled with peace.

And Patsy-O and Ita and their mother, of course, and the five faithful pets were as happy and as happy and as happy and as happy as the lovely days are

L   O   N   G

Anna-Maria McLean is a teacher from South East London. She has been working in schools [...] as a background in art and design with a BA Hons Degree in print media and surface design. H[...] the natural world was ignited by trips to the Horniman Museum and she remembers being intrigued by the many animals and birds in the bell cloche jars. Anna-Maria is passionate about caring for all creatures and has rescued and adopted many pets. She currently lives with her family including a cat called Paisley, two turtles called Dotty and Maria, a giant African Albino Land snail called Gary and a tank of tropical fish. She even saves snails, slugs and worms when they get in harm's way when it rains. Anna-Maria thinks it is very important to educate children about our amazing world and develop their vocabulary and has been told that her illustrations and writing should inspire the next generation of 'David Attenboroughs'.

A CIP catalogue record for this title is available from the British Library.

ISBN 9781398448698 (Paperback)
ISBN 9781398448704 (ePub e-book)

www.austinmacauley.com

First Published (2021)
Austin Macauley Publishers Ltd
25 Canada Square
Canary Wharf
London

Rianna Banana

And

Frances Bartlett AKA mum, for teaching me to love books.

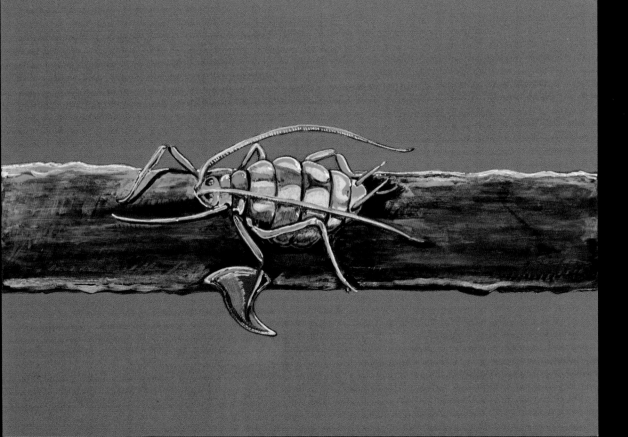

Aphids (Aphidoidea)

Aphids are an ant's close ally, excreting sugary juice.

The ants protect the aphids from the ladybirds on the loose.

The aphid would be eaten, if ants did not defend.

I never knew a greenfly, could be an ants best friend.

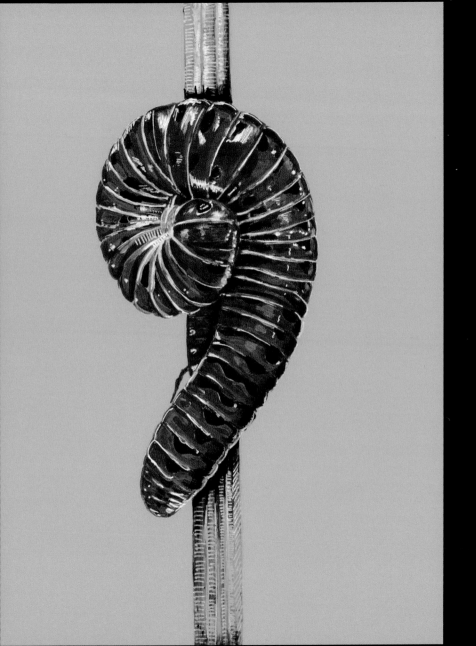

Millipede (Eurymerodesmus Spp)

Millipedes have a need for speed, they move on tiny feet

They curl they're fluid bodies which is also pretty neat.

With skeletons on the outside, and fleshy parts within.

When alarmed some millipedes exude toxins from their skin.

Their skin is armour plated; it protects them from attack

If it didn't have protection it would be eaten as a snack.

With rounded, sectioned bodies and antennae which are slender, this creature is elusive and a powerful defender.

This Arthropod is a noisy little guy; the males make such a noise when flying through the sky.

The females are much quieter and do not like to sing,

They lay their eggs on slits in plants, to keep their offspring in.

With bulging eyes and widespread wings they really are a dream.

They live for many, many years, some up to seventeen.

So if you see this little guy, do not be alarmed, he really is a cutie and full of true bug charm.

Bloody Nosed Beetle (Timarcha Tenebricosa)

Don't sneak up on this creature, you may be quite alarmed.

It squirts a bloody substance if it thinks it will be harmed.

The liquid comes out from its face, and tastes extremely foul.

To ward off would be predators, which may be on the prowl.

Its legs are long and slender, its body bulbous and round.

And though it looks like it can fly, it remains safely on the ground.

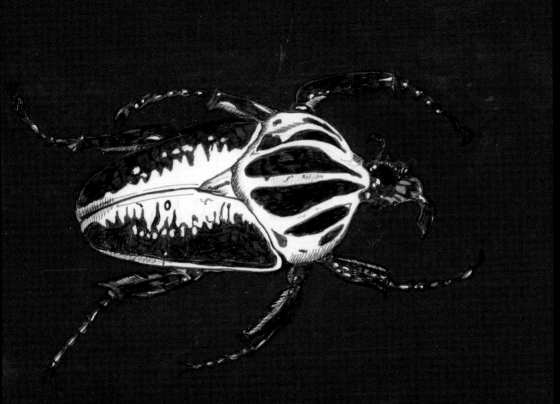

It munches on old vegetables and wood from rotting trees.

Because they keep the earth clean they must help prevent disease.

It even eats dung from animals, it's a super decomposer.

A natural and proficient garbage disposer.

Its cousin is the dung beetle a fellow sanitizer.

Flea (Siphonaptera)

Fleas are parasitic and hop from host to host,

They use their flattened bodies to move through fur they like the most.

The adults suck blood, whilst the babies eat their poo,

I bet you're glad you aren't a flea and I am quite glad too!

Coming out at night, to drink nectar from sweet smelling flowers.

Not competing with the butterfly, as they are out during daylight hours.

Their favourite plant is Honeysuckle and other tubular blooms.

They live in a range of places from grassland to sand dunes.

With pale green and soft pink wings, this creature has power and grace

Its proboscis is curled; it drinks

Green Stink bug

(Chinavia Hilaris)

Shaped like a shield with an armour plated frame.

It lives in woodlands and shrubs, it is also known by another name.

The shield bug eats many crops, by sucking sap and plant juice .

Watch out when barrel shaped eggs are laid, as soon babies will be on the loose.

Stink bugs have a secret weapon, to defend when under attack.

They let out a foul smelling odour from beneath their thorax tract.

A caterpillar predator, this may come as a surprise.

It does this by sneaking up, with a secretive guise.

So next time you see a stink bug do not be alarmed, it's only the size of a twenty pence piece.

It really won't cause you any harm. (Unless you are a caterpillar of course)

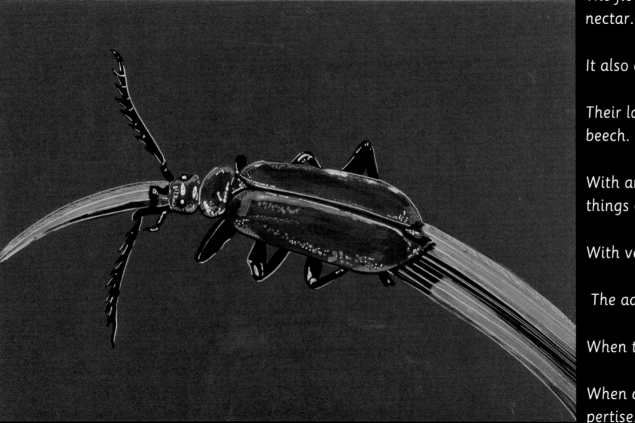

The flower longhorn beetle feeds on pollen and on nectar.

It also eats juicy fruit and is considered a pollinator.

Their larva bores into the bark of dying Elm and beech.

With antennae longer than its body, they can feel things out of reach.

With very narrow bodies and long and slender legs.

The adult finds a tree, in which to lay her eggs.

When they hatch the larva eat dead or decaying trees

When devouring rotting wood they show excellent ex-pertise.

Dragonfly (Antisoptera)

For around 300 million years, this master maneuverer
has been here.

Each wing moves independently and eyes move simultaneously.

This flying machine moves swiftly to target its prey; there
is little chance it is able to get away.

It focuses on a flying beast, a mosquito or butterfly on
which to feast.

Then it chases it until it is exhausted, unable to get away
it is totally accosted.

First ripping off its wings to incapacitate, no longer can
the victim circumnavigate.

On the fleshy parts it begins its dissection, crunching and
devouring the exoskeleton.

Dragonflies are superior, one of a kind, a greater insect
predator may be difficult to find!

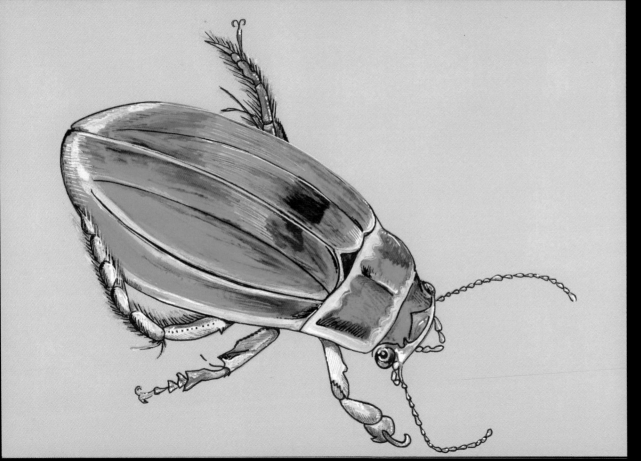

wetlands and streams, and places with lots of plant life, is the habitat of its dreams.

Nature's scuba diver, it breathes out of its butt, carrying a bubble of oxygen from spiracles near its gut.

Invertebrates, tadpoles and small fish are its prey, a prolific predator, there's no chance of getting away

The Larva catches tadpoles, they drink the fluids inside, So if you are a tadpole, you had better swim off and hide!

Common Garden Snail (Cornu Aspersum)

Snails are marvellous creatures they carry their home on their back.

They also use their shell to hide in, when they are under attack.

They eat most plant matter; gardeners think that they are pests.

But part of a vital life cycle; please treat them as more of a guest.

Simply relocate them by gently moving them on, don't hurt the little fellows; they're not doing anything wrong.

jaws.

They use them to fight off their rivals, when looking for girls they adore.

They begin, flying in summer, and at dusk they look for a mate.

They need to show who's the strongest, so that they can get a date.

When digging they burrow 50cm down, into rotting tree trunks or under the ground .

They build a cocoon like capsule, the size of an orange, quite round.

Females lay eggs in a cell of chewed wood and once they have hatched it becomes their food.

They live in these dwellings for up to three years, once they are ready to transition into adulthood.

Often taking up to three weeks to build underground, a safe, hidden haven by predators they can't be found

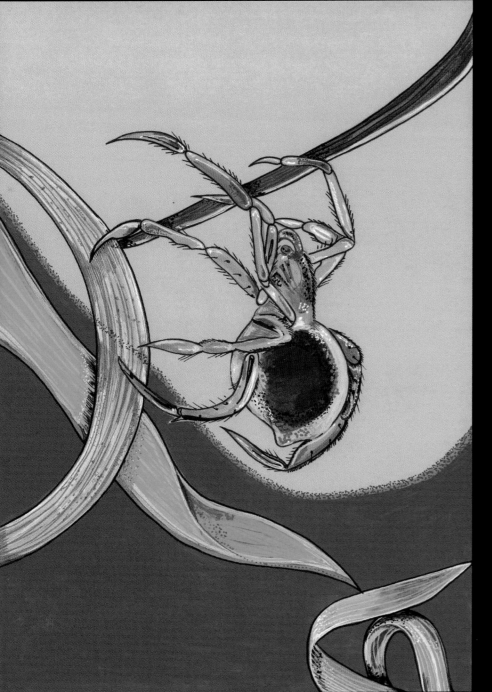

Water Spider (Argyroneta Aquatica)

The diving bell spider creates a capsule of air in a dome; it builds a bubble like structure, which it uses as its home.

By attaching silk to its thick abdomen hair, creating a large abode which it fills with air.

This super scuba diver creates an oxygen tank, when oxygen levels are as low as 10-20% in its storage bank.

This unique spider spends most of its life underwater, this multi-use vault is used for courtship, laying eggs, hibernation and slaughter.

These spiders prey on insects, mosquito larvae and Daphnia, once captured they will induce respiratory apnoea.

This clever *Argyroneta Aquatica* is a master of its craft, one of a kind this amazing arachnid is expertly able to engaft.

A single bee can fly up to the equivalent of 3 times around the globe, in order to make 1 pound of honey which is truly a feat on its own .

Well ,let me tell you something else that you will find hard to believe, bees can magically convert nectar into fructose and glucose which is not easy to achieve.

It has a special enzyme inside its tiny tum; it regurgitates the liquid and then passes it on to its chum.

The younger bee digests it and breaks it down even more, then regurgitated again it is almost ready to store.

But before it is, it needs a fan of thousands of fluttering wings, to create the right consistency and to give it that wonderful zing.

Once the honey is perfect, it gets placed into a store, with wax sealed at the entrance to keep it for a while more.

Earthworm (Lumbricina)

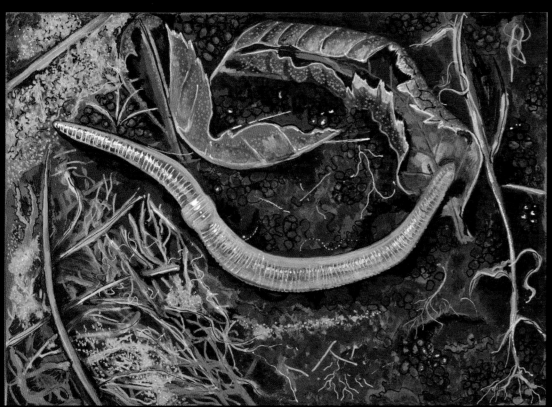

Earthworms are cold blooded invertebrates and must remain moist to stay alive.

They choose to live in humid, damp places with enough food sources to survive.

Baby worms hatch from cocoons, the size of a grain of rice.

Once they emerge from their casing they look just like mini adults how nice.

In order to keep on growing these little guys continue to moult.

This means as they grow they shed their skin and get bigger and bigger with each jolt.

Worms are delicate creatures that are sensitive to light.

Although you may see them during the day, they mostly come out at night.

They move to safety when they sense a predator moving near.

And dart back inside their burrow and swiftly disappear.

They process leaves and rotting food to produce some very rich soil.

Which such an important job to do I imagine their life is full of toil!

GLOSSARY

Abdomen - One of the main body parts of an insect which houses the heart, reproductive organs and digestive organs.

Abode - A place to live

Achieve - To successfully gain an objective

Accosted - To confront

Adore - To cherish

Alarmed – To become startled

Antlers – Chitin structures on the head used to defend (not the same as Deer antlers made from bone)

Antennae – appendages for sensing

Apnoea – A momentary lapse of breathing, especially during sleep

Arachnid – An eight legged creature with two body parts

Arthropod – A creature with jointed limbs and an exoskeleton

Armour – A protective covering

Bores – To create a hole

Bulbous – round or bulging

Capsule – A casing

Circumnavigate – To travel around the world

Competing – strive to be the best

Consistency - To keep something the same standard

Convert – To change something from one thing to another

Courtship - To find a mate

Curled - curved into a tight spiral

Daphnia - a tiny crustacean with a single eye

Defend/Defender-To protect itself or others

Decomposer- to facilitate decomposition (to help things break down)

Delicate – easily broken or damaged

Devouring – to eat completely

Digest – when food is eaten and processed

Disease- an illness or infection

Dissection- to cut something up

Dwelling - home

Elusive - keeps itself hidden

Emerge – move out or away from something to become visible

Engraft - to join or fasten

Entrance - an opening or a way in

Enzyme - a protein which causes a reaction

Equivalent – of the same value

Excreting - to expel or release

Exhausted - completely tired out

Exoskeleton - the outer protective casing

Expertise - skilfully

Expertly - highly skilled or knowledgeable

Extremely – to a very great degree

Exude - to release a liquid or scent

Favourite - liked more than any other

Flattened - make or become flat

Fluid - a substance with no fixed shape

Focuses - the centre of interest or activity

Fructose – a sugar of the hexose class found in honey and fruit

Glucose – a simple sugar which is an important energy source

Harmed – to physically injure

Hibernation – a condition or period when a plant or animal spends time during the winter in a dormant state

Host – an organism being attacked by a parasite

Incapacitate –deprived of strength or power

Independently – in a way that is free from outside influence

Invertebrate – an animal lacking a backbone

Jolt – push or shake abruptly

Liquid – a substance which flows freely

Magically – as if by magic

Majestic - grand

Maneuverer – a movement or series of movements

Marvellous – causing great wonder

Moult – to shed old feathers, hair or skin

Nectar – a sugary fluid secreted within flowers

Offspring – the young of an animal

Oxygen – One of the main elements that makes up air

Parasitic – living on another organism

Predator – an animal that eats other animals

Prevent – to keep something from happening

Proboscis - an elongated sucking mouthpart that is typically

Produces - to make something or bring something into existence

Protect – to keep safe from harm or injury

Prowl – to move stealthily especially in search of prey

Range - a variety of places/habitats

Regurgitate – bring up again to the mouth

Refiner – to remove impurities

Relocate – to change location

Respiratory - breathing

Rivals – a person or thing competing with another

Sanitizer – to cleanse and kill germs

Sealed – to prevent something from opening

Sectioned – to cut or separate into sections

Simultaneously – actions which happen at the same time

Skeleton – a rigid and supportive structure protecting the internal organs

Slaughter – to kill in an aggressive way

Slender – long and thin

Spiracles – an external respiratory opening

Substance – a particular kind of matter with uniform properties

Superior – higher in rank or status

Toil – to work extremely hard

Toxins - poisons

Transition – to change from one thing to another

Tubular – shaped like a tube

Unfurled – to uncurl

Vault - a large room or chamber

Vital – essential

Zing – energy/enthusiasm or liveliness

In Loving Memory of Dotty the Turtle and Gary the Giant African Land Snail.

You will be sadly missed.

R.I.P

2010—2023

2020—2023

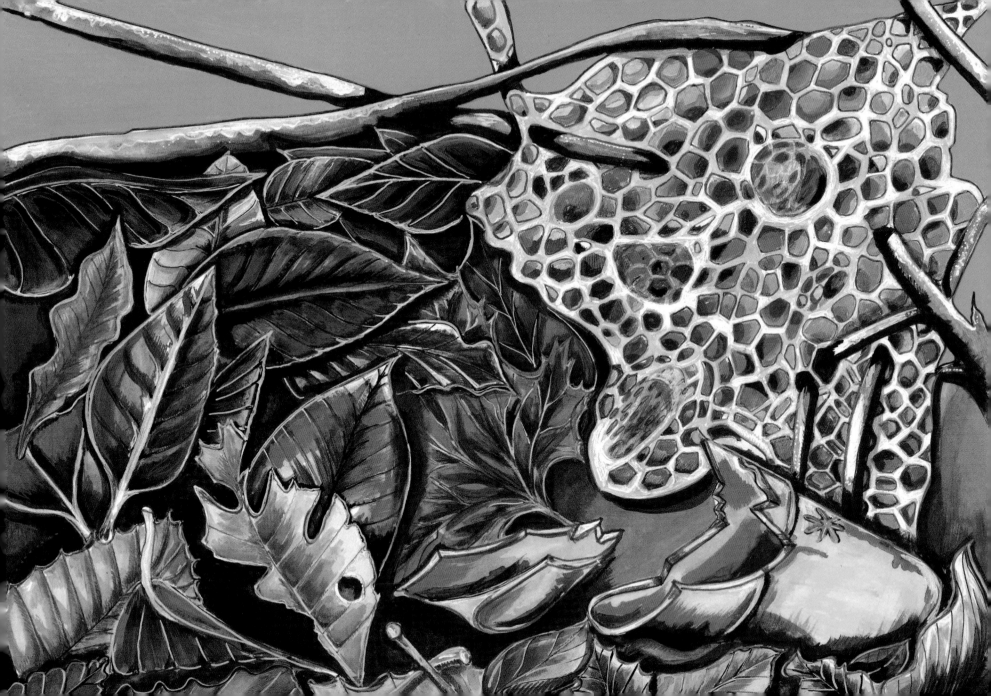